Universe 17

Universe 17

Edited by TERRY CARR

DOUBLEDAY & COMPANY, INC.

GARDEN CITY, NEW YORK

1987

Library of Congress Cataloging-in-Publication Data

Universe 17.

Contents: Second going/by James Tiptree, Jr.—
Mencken stuff/by Joel Richards—Lapidary nights/by
Marta Randall—[etc.]
1. Science fiction, American. I. Carr, Terry.
II. Title: Universe seventeen.
PS648.S3U539   1987   813'.0876'08   86–29281
ISBN: 0-385-23853-3

Contents

Universe 17

Science fiction writers have told us many a tale of humanity's first contact with alien beings from far stars; they've also made some fascinating speculations about religion. Here is an example of both: a wry novelette that introduces a race of aliens who have surprisingly practical ideas about gods.

James Tiptree, Jr.'s most recent books are Tales of the Quintana Roo *and* The Starry Rift.

SECOND GOING

by James Tiptree, Jr.

I didn't mean to start like this. I wanted to make it a nice formal Appendix, or Addendum, to the official Archives. The account of man's first contact with aliens: what really happened.

But I can't find any bound copies of the White Book, not even in the President's office. Except one somebody got mustard all over and another piece the rats got at. What I suspect, what I think is, *they never finished it.* All I can find is some empty cover-boxes, so I'm going to put these discs in one of those so people will know it's important.

After all, I am the official Archivist—I typed the promotion myself when Hattie went. I'm Theodora Tanton, Chief NASA Archivist. And I'm seventy-six years old, as of this morning. So is everybody, old—everybody who can remember, that is. So who's going to hear it, anyway? You with your six fingers or two heads or whatever?

You'll be around, though. They promised us that, that we wouldn't blow ourselves up. They said they fixed it. And I believe them. Not because I *believe* them exactly, but because I think they just might want to come back someday and find more than ashes.

They didn't command us not to fire atomic weapons, by the way. I guess they knew by that time that when a god commands Don't Eat Those Apples, or Don't Open This Box

—it's the first thing men'll do. (And manage to blame it on a woman, too, if you'll notice. But I digress.)

No, they just said, "We fixed that." Maybe the Russians have found out what they did by this time. Or the Israelis. What's left of the Pentagon is too scared to try. So, Hello, Posterity.

This is about what really happened, to add to the White Book, if you ever find one—ooops, that was a rat. I have a Coleman lantern, and a hockey stick for the rats.

Start with First Contact.

First Contact took place on Mars, with the men of the First Mars Mission. The two who had landed, that is. The command module pilot, Reverend Perry Danforth, was just flying orbits, looking down and seeing peculiar things. Meeting them on Mars confused everybody for a while. They were not Martians.

The best account of the meeting is from Mission Control. I found a man who had been a boy there, sort of a gofer. In that big room with all the terminals—you've seen it a million times on TV if you watched space stuff. So this first bit is dictated live by Kevin (Red) Blake, now aged 99.5 years.

But before him I want to say a word about how everything was. *So normal.* Nothing sinister or dramatic going on. Like in a ship that's slowly, very slowly, listing to one side, only nobody's mentioning it. That's all underneath. But little things give it away, like this one Kevin told me before they landed.

It was a long trip, see, two years plus. They were all in the command module, called *Mars Eagle.* James Aruppa, commanding, and Todd Fiske, and the Reverend Perry, who wasn't going to get to land. (Personally, I'd have broken Todd's arm or something, if I'd been Perry, so I could get to land. Imagine getting so close—and then flying circles for a week while the others are on *Mars!* But he acted perfectly happy about it. He even made a joke about being "the most expensive valet parking service ever." Very cooperative and one-for-all, the Reverend. I never did find out exactly what he was the Reverend of; maybe it was only a nickname.)

Anyway about five or six months out, at a time when they were supposed to be fast asleep, they called Mission Control. "Are you all right back there?"

"Sure, everything's nominal here. What's with you?"

Well, it turned out that they'd seen this flash, some trick rock reflection or something that made a burst of light right where Earth was. And they thought it was missiles, see, World War III starting . . . anybody would've, in those days. That's what I mean by the feelings just underneath. But nobody ever said a gloomy word, on top.

There were other things underneath, of course, different for different people, all adding up to The End. But this is no place to talk about the old days; it's all changed now. So that's that, and now here comes Kevin:

"I can remember it like it was yesterday. All morning had been occupied with the Lander carrying Todd and Jim Aruppa coming down and finding a flat place. I nearly got thrown out of the control room for sticking my head in people's way to catch a glimpse of a screen while I was bringing stuff. The amount of coffee those NASA boys put away! And some of them ate—one man ate seven egg sandwiches—they were all keyed up like crazy. All right, I'll stick to the point. I know what you want to hear.

"So by then it was coming pitch dark on Mars, only the Lander's lights glaring on a pebbly plain with cracks in it. The computer colored it red, I guess it was. Mission Control wouldn't let them get out then. They were ordered to sleep until it got full light again. Ten hours. . . . Imagine, *sleeping* your first night on Mars!

"The last thing was, Perry up in the command module reported a glow of light on the eastern horizon. It wasn't a moon rising—we'd already seen one of those. A little greenish crescent, going like crazy.

"So during the night Perry was supposed to check on what might be glowing toward the east—a volcano, maybe? But by the time he came around to where he could see the place again, the glow had faded to nearly nothing, and next trip there was nothing at all to see.

"At this time a relief crew was on the CRTs in Mission Control, but every so often one of the men who were supposed to be sleeping in their quarters next door would come in and just stare at the screens for a few minutes. All you could see was a faint, jagged horizon line, and then the stars began.

"First light was supposed to be at 5:50 A.M. our time (see, I even remember numbers!) and by that time the whole day crew was back in the room, everybody all mixed together, and all wanting coffee and Danishes.

"On the screens the sky was getting just a little lighter, so the horizon looked sharper and darker until suddenly a faint lightness came on the ground plain in front of the mountains. And then came a minute I'll never forget. Like the whole room was holding its breath, only whispering or rustling a little around their dark screens. And then Eggy Stone yelled out loud and clear:

" *'There's something there! It's big! Oh, man!'*

"That made it official, what the sharp-eyed ones thought they'd been picking up but couldn't believe, and everybody was jabbering at once. And the voices of the astronauts cutting through everything, with that four-and-a-half-minute lag, about how this Thing was sitting in front of them unlit, unmoving, no indication of how it had come there, whether it crawled or flew in or bored up out of the ground. Of course, they thought it was Martians.

"What it was was a great big, say fifty-meter-long, dumbbell shape lying there about a hundred meters in front of their main window. It was two huge spheroids, or hexasomethings, connected by one big fat center bar—really like a dumbbell. Only in the middle of the connection was a chamber, say three meters each way. We could see right in because its whole front side was folded back like a big gull-wing door. It appeared to be padded inside. The computer called it light blue, with two rust-colored lumps like cushion seats back on the floor inside.

"And both of the big dumbbell chambers at the ends had like windows spaced all around them.

"And filling the window of the end nearest us, the window we could see into, was something moving or flickering slightly, something shiny and lighter blue. It took a second or two to recognize it, because of its size—it was over a meter long, almost round.

"It was an eye. A great, humongous, living eye, blue with a white rim. And looking at us.

"Like the creature it belonged to was so big it was all curled up inside its compartment, with its eye pressed to the glass. For some reason, right from the start we knew that the creature, or being, or whatever, had only one central eye.

"In addition to looking at us—that is, at the camera—most of the time, the eye was also swiveling to examine the Lander and everything around.

"Now all through the excitement Todd and Jim in the Lander were trying to tell us something. I wasn't in on this, but whenever I could get near Voice Contact I heard things like, 'We are not crazy! I tell you we are not crazy; it's talking in our heads. *Yes*, in English. We get two words very distinctly: *peace* and *welcome*. Over and over. And we are not out of our minds; if I could figure a way to get this on the caller you'd hear—'

"They sounded madder and madder. I guess Mission Control was giving them a hard time, especially General Streiter, who was sure it was a Soviet Commie trick of some kind. And of course there was no way for them to get a mental voice on the antennae. But then the aliens apparently solved that for themselves. Just as Jim was saying for the tenth time that he wasn't crazy or hadn't drunk too much coffee, all our communications went blooie for a minute and then this great big quiet voice drowned everything.

" 'PEACE . . .' it said. And then, 'WELL-COME!'

"Something about the voice, its tone, made Mission Control sound for a minute like a—well, like a cathedral. 'PEACE! . . . WELCOME! . . . PEACE . . . FRIENDS . . .' "

"And then it added, very gentle and majestic, 'COME . . . COME . . .'

"And Mission Control became aware that Todd and Jim were preparing to go out of the Lander.

"Pandemonium!

"Well, I'll skip all this bit where Mission Control was ordering them to stay inside, on no account to even put a hand out, to unsuit—Jim and Todd were calmly suiting up—and anything else they could think of and General Streiter ordering court-martials for everybody in sight, on Mars or Earth—it even went so far as getting the President out of bed to come and countermand them in person. I found out afterward that the poor man got so mixed up he thought they were *refusing* to go out onto Mars, and he was supposed to tell them to! And all with this four-and-a-half-minute lag, and this great hushy voice blanking everything out with 'PEACE . . . WELCOME . . .'

"Until finally it was obvious even to the general that nothing could be done, that forty-four million miles away two Earthmen were about to walk out onto Mars and confront The Alien."

(This is Theodora putting in a word here. See, everyone had been so convinced that there was no life on Mars above something like lichen that absolutely no instructions had been thought up for meeting large-scale sentient life, let alone with telepathic communications.)

"Well, they evacuated the air, and as they went to go down the ladder, Jim Aruppa grabbed Todd, and we could hear him saying in his helmet, 'Remember, you bastard! Count cadence *now!*'

"And nobody knew what that was until we found out there'd been this private arrangement between the two men. After all those months together, see, Jim wasn't going to take all the glory for being the First Man on Mars. As he put it to Todd, 'Who was the *second* man to step onto the moon?' And Todd had to guess twice, and nobody else knew either. And Jim wasn't going to let that happen again. So he ordered Todd to descend in sync with him and make an absolutely simultaneous first-foot-down. That was one of the little squabbles that kept Mission Control lively all those two years. Some kind of guy, Jim.

"So there they were counting cadence down the ladder to Mars—to *Mars*, man!—with this alien Thing a hundred yards away staring at them.

"And they walked over to it slowly and carefully, looking at everything, the eye following them. And there were no signs of how it had possibly moved there except by some kind of very gentle flight. But no machinery, nothing at all but these two big hexagonal spheroids with windows. And the compartment between. The first word Jim sent back was, 'It seems to be entirely non-metallic. Not plastic, either. More like a—like a smooth shiny dry pod, with windows set in. The frames are non-metallic too.'

"And then they got to where they could see the windows on the farther-off spheroid—and there was another eye looking out at them from it!

"It seemed exactly like the first eye, only slightly larger and paler. The flesh around the eyes registered blue too, by the way—and there was no sign of eyelashes.

"And then both Jim and Todd claimed that this eye *winked* at them and Mission Control went back to calling them crazy.

"When they got back in front, by the open compartment, they made signals as though they were hearing something. And then the voice we could hear via radio changed too. 'Come,' it said in sort of grand-friendly tones. 'Come. . . . Please come in. Come with, say hello friends.'

"Well, that sent Mission Control into a new spasm of countercommands, in the midst of which the two men set the camera on its tripod outside, and walked into the open alien compartment, bouncing a little on the padded floor. Then they turned around to face us, and sat down on the seat-cushion-looking things. And at that the big overhead door slid smoothly forward and down and closed them in. It had a window in it—in fact it was mostly window. But before anybody could think of any reaction to *that*, it opened up again halfway, and Todd and Jim stepped out. Four and a half minutes later we heard, 'They say to bring food for one day.'

"And the man went back up into the Lander to collect supplies.

"Somehow the ordinariness, or what you might call considerateness of this just took the wind out of a lot of angry lungs.

" 'No water necessary, they say,' Jim Aruppa told us as they climbed back out of the Lander. 'But we brought some just in case. I never thought I'd be glad to see a can of Tab.' He grinned, holding up his little camp basin. 'But we can at least wash our hands in it.'

" 'Jeez, it's getting like a god-forsaken *picnic!*' Eggy Stone shouted over the general uproar.

"Well, the door snapped over and shut down again. We could see them through the window, waving. And then the thing simply lifted up quietly and flew like magic toward and over the camera, and over the Lander, and we couldn't pick it up again. And that was absolutely all for thirty-six long hours, until—

"—Say, Miz Tanton, haven't you got the tape of what they said when they came back? I just can't talk one word more."

So here's a break. All this next part I put together from Jim and Todd's report-tapes of their trip, plus the officially cleaned-up version of it that was in the *Times*. I found a stack of archive tape dupes in the janitor's cubby.

But before that, I should say that the Reverend Perry had been busy, up in the Martian sky. Mission Control at least had one astronaut who would take orders, and they'd told him to try to check out where the Thing had come from during the night. So he got busy with his 'scopes and sensors, and about the time Jim and Todd were going back for their chow, he had a report. A Martian building, or structure, "like a big mound of bubbles," was located in the foothills of Mount Eleuthera to the east. But as a city it was strange—it had no suburbs, no streets, not much internal differentiation, and no roads leading to or away. (Of course not; we know now it was a ship.)

So when the flying dumbbell bearing the two humans went off NASA's cameras, Perry knew where to try to pick them up. And by the way, although Perry was obedient to orders, he too was acting strange. He didn't volunteer anything, but on direct questioning he admitted that he was hearing voices in his head—at first he said something about a 'ringing in his ears'—and when the aliens' voices cut in on the radio wavelength, Perry pulled himself down to his knees and NASA could see enough to realize he was both trying to pray and weep. This didn't disturb them overmuch —considering what else was going on—because the Reverend was known to indulge in short prayers whenever some special marvel of space came up, and he was addicted to brief thanksgivings at any lucky break. He was quite unselfconscious about this, and it never interfered with his efficiency, so maybe NASA figured they were covering all bets by having him along. General Streiter asked him if he was all right.

"I shall say no more about this now, General," Perry replied. "I recognize it is inappropriate to this phase of our mission. But I sincerely believe we have contacted a . . . a Higher Power, and that some very great good may come of this if we prove worthy."

Streiter took this in silence; he knew Perry as a congenial fellow Commie-hater, and he had expected him to see Red skulduggery in the sudden materialization of the Thing. But Perry seemed to be taking another tack; the general respected him enough to let him be.

So back to Todd and Jim, who were being flown silently, magically, over the Martian landscape. They were at the big door-window. The lift-off was so gentle that Jim said he wouldn't have known they were moving if he hadn't been looking out. This reassured them about the absence of any straps or body-holds in the padded compartment they had entered.

They were of course looking for a city or town, or at least the openings of tunnels, and the 'mound of bubbles' Perry was reporting took them by surprise. Near the top of the mound was an opening where a sphere or two seemed to be missing; as they came over it, they saw that their craft exactly fitted in. Forward motion ceased quietly, and with a soft, non-metallic brushing sound the modules that carried them dropped into the empty slots. Todd was inspired. "Hey, that's all one huge ship—and this is a dinghy!"

His mind had broadcast the right picture. "Yess!" the aliens chorused, "our ship!"

Before they could see anything of the interior, a side window in their compartment opened, and a light blue, leathery-looking trunk or tentacle about the size of a fire hose appeared. "Hello!" said the voice in their heads clearly.

"Hello," they said aloud.

The tentacle extended itself towards Jim's hand. Involuntarily he drew back. "Hello? Hello? Friends!" said the soundless voice. "Touch?"

Gingerly Jim extended his hand, and to his surprise, after a little confusion, the contact the alien wanted was achieved.

"It wants to shake hands!" Jim exclaimed to Todd.

"Yes! Friends! Shake!" And a similar window in the opposite wall opened, revealing the other alien. Its tentacle was larger, more wrinkled, and lighter blue. "Friends?"

A round of enthusiastic handshaking ensued. Then the second alien wanted something more. Its tentacle's tip pulled clumsily but gently at Todd's glove, and he got a confused message about taking it off and speaking.

When Todd got his glove off and took the alien's flesh barehanded, he gasped and seemed to stagger.

"What's wrong? Todd?"

"Okay—it's okay, very—. Try it."

Jim ungloved and grasped the tip of the alien limb. Then he too gasped—as contact occurred, there came with it a rush of communication, both verbal and pictorial, in which he could pick out bits or sequences of past events, present communication, speculations, images—including a vision of himself—plans, questions—he was all but *inside* an alien mind!

They were both laughing, delighted at this immense novelty to explore—and from the other sides of their padded walls came echoing chuckles. A pleasant fragrance like cinnamon was coming through their air filters, too. They were the first humans to smell the spicy odor emitted by these aliens when excited and interested.

"This is going to take practice," Jim gasped. He tried to convey the idea to the alien whose blue tentacle he was clasping, and received a strong feeling of assent. Delicately, it moved its tentacle within his grip, so that only certain surfaces were apposed, and the rush of mindflow quieted down.

Then it tapped his palm in a way that they soon came to recognize as meaning "I have something to tell/show you." And he found himself seeing a connected, coherent 'movie' of the alien's bubble-craft approaching Earth sometime earlier, sampling the airborne communications—both radio and video—and selecting the large land mass of North America to linger near. "All same language," said the voice in his head. "Many pictures—teach much." And then a sample of what they had set themselves to learn—recognizable segments of "Dallas," "All My Children," "Sesame Street," newscasts—and ads, ads, ads unceasing. "Much do not understand."

Whew! Jim tried to interrupt, but the flow went on. From it he gathered that the aliens had evoked a few hostile reactions from U.S. Air Force installations. Also the aliens soon learned that great intergroup hostilities existed on Earth. They had actually been on the verge of leaving—"Go look better planet"—when they learned about the Mars mission. It seemed to them that this would be the ideal place and way to meet humanity. So here they were, and here were our two astronauts—deep in converse, without having seen the forms or faces of their new friends. (For from the start, there had seemed to both men no question that a *friendly* meeting was in progress, and friendship was growing between them every moment.)

"Now you want say Hello others, so we talk more?"

"Yes indeed."

A picture sequence in their minds prepared them and then the whole back wall of their compartment irised open, giving onto a great, softly glowing space. When they went to it they saw that the "mound of bubbles" was actually a shell around an open core; all the "bubbles" gave onto a common open space, in which were a few structures whose use or meaning they couldn't guess. All around the walls, ceiling, floor were the openings of compartments similar to their own, some brightly lighted, some dim, some dark, so that the whole formed a kind of grand auditorium or meeting hall. At the mouths of nearly every individual compartment was an alien, or two or more, all with their great single eyes turned eagerly in their direction.

And here I have to pause, or put in asterisks or somehow prepare you before I describe what you notice I've omitted so far—the aliens' shapes.

The color of course you know—sky blue in the main, with here and there blues lighter or darker, from slate to peacock blue, from pale blue foam to deep marine. And the great eyes were quite human-shaped, though the size of footlockers. And the tentacles you have met—each had groups of sucker-discs which were apparently quiescent unless the owner wished to cling.

It is their general shape you don't yet know.

There is one, and only one, Earthly animal that they resembled, and they resembled it very closely. To put it bluntly, the aliens looked like gigantic cerulean octopuses.

Imagewise, of course, it was terrible.

In addition to being unspellable (octopusses, octopuses, octopoi, octopi, octopodes?), it conjured up every old horror cliché. And it was undeniable—they *were* in fact simply big, air-breathing octopuses; we all learned later that they had evolved in their planet's oceans, and slowly adapted to land as their oceans dried. Their mantles had lost the propulsive function, and four of their back tentacles had evolved to limbs suitable for walking on land, leaving the other four to take on hand-and-arm and telepathic transmission abilities.

Their heads were large and bald and shiny above the

single eye, and their mantles began where a chin should be, concealing their noses and mouths, or beaks, or whatever. Also to be glimpsed beneath the mantle's rippling edges was a mass of darker blue furlike organs, among which seemed to be some very small, delicate tentacles of unknown use.

In all, had it not been for their truly lovely coloring and odor and the expressive friendliness of their large eyes, the first impression of the aliens to a human, would have to be revulsion bordering on terror.

The Earthly media of course went wild at first—GIANT BLUE OCTOPUSES ON MARS! shrilled even the staidest. Octopus!—the name alone makes for the world's worst PR. That's why I've given you all this preliminary stuff, instead of just dictating from the newsclips.

The photos, when they came, made things a little better, because their postures were so versatile and graceful. And their basically radial bodies were obviously in transition to a bilaterally symmetrical form—the four "back" leg-tentacles were much larger and longer, to free the front four. In fact if —as happened later—a small one wore a long robe with a hood to conceal the shiny bald dome above the eye, it could pass for a large somewhat top-heavy human form. And they spent much of their time thus upright, looking rather like multiply armed Indian deities, and smelling delightful. So that, as soon as Earth saw more of them, the original "sci-fi" horror images were seen to be ludicrously inappropriate, and were forgotten.

While Todd and Jim were taking in the nature of their audience, and vice versa, their new friends were folding back the walls of their compartments and dragging the cushions to the edge of the front.

"We speak one-to-all like this. We show you." And they motioned Todd and Jim to take seats. "No fear fall off, everybody catch."

Then they stationed themselves on each side, laid their transmission-tentacles across Jim's and Todd's shoulders, and seemed to listen.

"No—clothes too thick. Can take off, please? Air good

here." So the men first gingerly lifted off their helmets—getting a real blast of carnation scent—and then started peeling down. They felt a bit odd about it in front of all those eager eyes, but what the hell, their bodies were no more to the aliens than a wombat's to them. So they sat back down again, nude, and the tentacles came back. "Ahhh! Good!"

And with that the two big aliens stretched their other transmitter arms out to the aliens in the compartments next door, and these did the same to those around them, so that in a minute the whole great amphitheater was intricately laced together, with the men as foci.

While this was happening, Todd felt a plucking at his shins. He looked down, and there was this dark blue tentacle coming up at him from the compartment below. He heard, or sensed, what could only be a giggle, and next instant three big round bright eyes were staring up at him over the edge of his floor. A spicy fume of interest wafted up.

The alien next to him emitted a reproving sound, and batted at the eyes with a spare limb. "Young ones!" Peering down, Todd and Jim saw a cluster of smaller aliens in the chamber below, evidently trying to get in on the network by short circuit. "It's okay." He grinned. "No problem to us."

So their two big friends let the little fellows sneak tendrils in to touch the men's legs and feet.

"Okay . . . you go first?" said the one next to Jim. "Oh, wait. Us name Angli. An-gli," it repeated aloud. "You name?"

"Hello, Angli!" said Jim to them both. "Us name hu-mans. But"—he pointed at the other—"you have special personal name, for you only?"

Well, that was their introduction to the one great difficulty of mind-speech—asking questions. It took minutes for them to get sorted out as individuals, and even so they weren't sure they had it right. Jim said, "The customary thing here seems to be to call up a quick flash-image of the person, or his eye, or something special about him or her. I don't think verbal names are used much. But our friends seem to be something like Urizel and Azazel, for what it's worth. We'll try calling them that and see if it works." Then he put his arm around Todd. "We together, hu-mans," he said. "But *he* alone"—gesturing—"is *Todd*. I—me, here—am *Jim*. Todd . . . Jim. Jim . . . Todd. Get it?"

"Me Jane, you Tarzan," muttered Todd.

"Shut up, you idiot, this is no time to clown. We'll have to be sure somehow that they know what a joke is. All right. Urizel, Azazel, and all the rest of you Angli—what do you want to know about us humans first?"

And so started the greatest show-and-tell anthropology class of their lives.

Surprisingly soon, it got itself organized with their two friends alternately passing questions to the men. Not surprisingly, in view of their TV fare, the first queries were mainly about economics. Todd had the pleasure of trying to answer, "What is 'money?' " He managed to form a picture of a medium of exchange passing from hand to hand in the human world. And luckily, the Angli seemed to have something to relate this to; Jim got a visual image of furry brown creatures carrying on their tails stacks of big square things with holes in them that had to be clumsy coins.

"Gosh, what does a really rich one do?" Todd didn't expect an answer, but the Angli had picked up the drift of his query, and he got a clear mental picture of a pompous-looking brown alien followed by a formal train of specialized coin-bearers, their long tails erect and loaded to the tips with big discs.

Both humans and Angli laughed.

"What do you do with money?" Azazel asked. Jim gulped and tried to visualize a bank teller, vaults, checkbooks.

"I fear I'm not doing justice to the international banking system," he said to Todd. "But, dammit, ours has to make more sense than carrying your money around on your tail!"

"I'm beginning to wonder," Todd muttered. "No, no," he said to Azazel, "Not important."

It was now very apparent that the humans were by no means the first new race the Angli had met. Fleeting images of many other aliens, worlds, cities, ships, crossed their per-

ceptions from various Angli minds. These aliens seemed to
have spent years jaunting about the galaxy, meeting people
and things.

As to the Angli's own home world—the notion that they
were Martians was disposed of very early—they were shown
an image of a planet not unlike Earth, but greener, near a
GO-type sun. A view of the nearby constellations enabled
the men to guess that it was near the nebula in Orion's
sword. A close-up view showed a lush, attractive landscape
with a bubble-dome town.

And the Angli were not alone! Another intelligent race
lived there—no, wait, *had* lived there once—"many times
ago." The blurred image of a porpoiselike creature with legs
seemed to have passed through many minds. "They go"—
but whether they had left or died off was never clear; these
Angli perhaps didn't know. The Angli were alone there now.

One last fact that came out was sensational: the "bubbles"
the men were in wasn't their only ship. They had maybe half
a dozen ships and stuff parked on Luna, on the back side of
our moon, where we couldn't see them. One or more contained a lot more Angli, who wanted simply to sleep until a
really promising planet was found. ("Wake us when we get
someplace!") Very young Angli were also asleep there. Another one—or more—contained members of another race,
whose planet had been in trouble, so the Angli volunteered
to find them a new one. (In their experience, the galaxy
seemed to be full of all kinds of planets just waiting to be
found.) This particular race needed an aquatic environment,
it seemed.

Another ship seemed to contain assorted seeds and supplies; despite their casual behavior, the Angli really had
great practical sense about essentials. And at least two were
empty—one had contained a race the Angli had successfully
relocated. And a final one contained a spectacular cargo we
on Earth were soon to get a view of.

(Of course, on learning that other ships existed, the general and others promptly began to suspect that the Angli also
had battleships or other military capabilities parked up

there, and many covert plans were laid to sneak around Luna and peek. But they all came to nothing, and nothing hostile ever showed up.)

Each query raised a dozen others; the hours passed like minutes. Finally a growing emptiness in their middles forced the men to call a halt.

"We eat now?"

The Angli too, it seemed, were tired and hungry, although so fascinated that they seemed ready to go on indefinitely. But at Jim's question a cheer broke out among the young ones below. In no time they had produced great baskets of what looked like hardtack, and were carrying them around the auditorium, passing a container out to each row. Each Angli in turn helped him- or herself to a piece, and tucked it neatly under a mantle fold in their central bodies, where the men had surmised their mouths, or beaks, might be.

"We've got to get this gender business straightened out," Todd said with his mouth full. "Oh, cripes. How do we do *that*, Tarzan?"

"Maybe we don't, until we can produce a real Jane." And so it turned out. He seemed to evoke a response to his first tries at describing human sexes—"Humans like Jim and me here"—he indicated his genitalia—"we call 'men.' Other humans have lumps *here* but not *here*—we call them 'women.' And it takes the two kinds together to make young ones." Todd continued, "How do you make young?"

But here all impression of understanding faded, and an Angli question, "What you call Mathlon?" stumped everybody. Mind-visions of an Angli picking things out of a puddle didn't help.

Theodora Tanton here again. I just excerpted all that above from Jim's long report, to give the atmosphere and show some of the problems; I guess that some parts belong in the after-lunch session. And don't shoot me, sisters, about the gender part and the "lumps"—that's just what the man said. I put most dialogue as if it were ordinary speech instead of explaining whether it was telepathy or audible speech each time. Men and Angli were developing a sort of half-speech/half-thought lingo that worked well.

The afternoon, or what was left of it, went as fast as the morning, and soon the sunlight that filtered through into the great central dome was visibly reddening into a typical Martian sunset.

"We go back now, please," the men said. "Our people have much fear."

"Ohh-kayee!" said Urizel, and they all laughed. One thing the men couldn't get over was how human their laughter was—and they thought ours was incredibly Anglian.

So they closed up the doors, the humans suited up, the module lifted away silently from its slot, and the trip repeated itself in reverse. They tried again—it had come up all day—to understand the source of its power, but always the same answer baffled them. "We do with bodies. Like so—" and the speaker would loft himself a few meters, apparently effortlessly, and descend again. "You no do, eh? We find many races no do; only one we find can do." And a picture came in their minds of a large, raylike being, sailing and flapping above an alien landscape. The Angli tapped his head regretfully. "Fly pretty, but not have much brain. Come later, maybe."

Now on their return trip they could see their friends loading in, and it was obvious that they propelled their craft by simply *pushing* it up from inside, as a man under a table might lift it with his back—but with no need to press down on anything. Nor did it seem tiring.

"Antigravity is the best guess we can make," Jim told Earth later.

One more item they were shown: in both the end compartments was a window in the floor, beside which was a bank of what turned out to be outside lights, including infrared. They were powered by small batteries.

"Use up fast," Azazel said, frowning. And they didn't turn the lights on again until they were over the Earth Lander. This contraption was the first construction of metal or wires the men had seen. It looked handmade. "We get from special people," Azazel said, and transmitted a brief shot of some sort of aliens in an apparent workshop. "Not on our home."

"We make light too," Urizel said, and from under his (or her) mantle suddenly came a soft blue glow, which brightened to a point, then turned off. "Is work," the big Angli said expressively. Light was evidently strictly for emergency use. They seemed to have fantastically good night vision; the men suspected that their use of the floodlights as they neared the Lander was more for the Earthmen's sake than their own. "You no see so good in dark."

"Maybe they were surprised when we didn't seem to see their approach last night," Jim said.

And then it was time to say goodbye and get back in their own little craft. And report to Mission Control.

"I bet they don't let us off the hook for hours and hours and hours," Todd said. And he was proved right. Kevin remembers vividly the shout that rang through Mission Control when the camera picked up their approaching lights. And then it took half the night to relay and record what I've put down here, plus a lot of repeats and mix-ups I've cut out.

Oh—I've forgotten one big thing. Just as they were leaving the dome a senior-looking Angli sent them a message through Azazel.

"He say, why not we take you home to Earth? Go quick, like maybe thirty-forty your days. We get human now up in sky, leave your ships here, you come back and get some other time. And you help us say Hello and make friendship with Earth?"

What an offer! "And with a soft landing at the end," crooned Todd ecstatically.

"Tell him yes, most happy," replied Jim. "Say—is he your leader?"

Now that brings up another subject I've been postponing —their government. As far as we ever found out, they virtually had none. The older Angli formed a loose set of council that anybody who wanted to could be in. Any question, like where to go next, or what to do about a specific problem, was apparently solved by informal mind-melding. People would put up ideas, and they'd be mulled over until a consensus evolved. What happened in the event of a serious disagreement? But there doesn't seem to have been any. "Oh, we take turns," said Azazel negligently.

Anyway, thus it was that the great homecoming of our successful Mars mission was in an alien ship in no way under the control of NASA, although they politely accepted all our communications. And they seemed surprised at the close supervision expected from and by Mission Control. On their home world, apparently, people just wandered hither and yon, off to a moon, or whatever.

One of the rites of growing up, it seemed, was making your own vehicle (they were indeed gigantic dried seed pods) and fitting it out for long trips. With their long-range mind-speech capability, there were no problems about getting lost, and their world seemed to have had few dangers. About the only mishap that seemed likely to occur to young ones jaunting about was when their presence or chatter annoyed some elder citizen who would complain to the council and have them grounded for a week or two. Like youngsters everywhere, they prized mobility and were always putting in work improving their craft, which virtually served as alternate homes. The climate, one gathered, was very benign.

It sounded idyllic; I wasn't the only one to start to wonder why, really, they had left. . . .

The day of their arrival on Earth has been so amply covered in schoolbooks that I have only small pieces to add, like about the riot. What went on at first was all standard—this great beige bubble-nest wafting down toward a cleared-off area in a sea of people, escorted for the last miles by practically everything the Air Force could put in the air. It sat down resiliently and before it had finished heaving, Angli all over the top began opening doors and looking out. A group escorting the three astronauts got out together and flew them down to where a cordoned and carpeted way to the receiving stand was marked off.

There were Urizel and Azazel, and a pair of aged senior councilors the men had persuaded to come along. Their progress was highly informal; people could see that the men were trying to report back to their Commander-in-Chief in a stylish, military way, but the Angli were hard to keep in line. They began thought-broadcasting to the crowd in general, right over the heads of the officials. And then they hooked into the PA system with "Hello! Peace! Friends!" And the press corps broke the lines by the ship and began infiltrating everywhere. Kevin was with the NASA Press contingent; he passed me a few tidbits. And the aged councilors, to whom one Earthman was much like another, began greeting the police and Secret Service men who were standing, arms linked, with their backs to the ship, trying to contain the swaying crowd. And during the official party's slow progress to the stand, Angli began coming out of the ship and making short flights over the heads of the crowd.

The stage was set for trouble, and it happened—five or six dark blue young Angli came out together with their arms full of something and flew over the crowd to the right, looking for a place to land and calling out "Friends!" and laughing that human laugh. What they had was blooms from the ship's hydroponics—big, fragrant stalks that unfortunately looked a bit like hand grenades. The crowd was too thick below them, so they began dropping the flowers onto people's heads. At that, the humans below started to mill, some people backing away in alarm while others pressed forward curiously. And the youngsters circled close overhead, laughing and pelting people with flowers.

Suddenly someone took real fright, and a small local stampede away from the Angli started. Others, seeing people running and feeling themselves pushed, began to run and push aimlessly too. Shouting broke out. The pushing intensified fast—and a woman screamed and went down.

All this showed only as a confused place on the edge of the TV screens, while the astronauts and the Angli were still straggling up the cordoned pathway to the stand where the presidential party was waiting. As the sound of shouting rose from off-screen, the United States Marine Band broke into a louder march piece, which amplified the confusion over an outbreak of real screaming and yells.

Urizel, sensing what was happening, dropped Todd's arm and flew over the tangle with the idea of shooing the youngsters back to the ship. But the arrival of this monster of much greater size frightened more people. The fallen woman was trampled and began to shriek. Urizel, spotting her, dived to the spot and sent his long tentacles down to extricate her, really scaring the people nearby.

About then, police sirens started up, an ambulance got its warbler going and began pressing into the scene. This excited more people outside the immediate nucleus. Some tried to gather their families and run, while others ran toward the uproar. The yelling developed a panicky, ominous beat. Meanwhile, those on the red carpet were still making their slow way to the President on the stand.

Now, every telepathic race is well aware of the terrible danger of contagious panic, the threat of a mind-storm. Both inside the ship and out, the Angli became aware of what was going on, and about to get much worse. Their response was automatic.

In perfect synchrony, they all stopped whatever they were doing, and sent out a united, top-power mental command: *"Quiet! Be calm! Sleep!* . . . QUIET! BE *CALM! SLEEP!"* It blasted the field.

So powerful was this thought-command that by the first repetition the yells and shouts died in people's throats. The uproar tapered down to a strange silence, in which the band raggedly played on for a few bars before they too were overwhelmed. Running people slowed to a walk, to a standstill; their heads drooped, and they saw the ground looking invitingly comfortable, attracting them to relax down. And suddenly, all in the moments that the great command silently went out, what had been a wildly agitated mob became a field of peaceful sleepers. Some slept sitting with their heads on their knees, others sprawled full length, their heads on any neighboring body.

The police and Secret Service men were of course affected too, and after a moment's heroic resistance, they went down in waves atop their sleeping charges.

The band and the PA system were silent, and on the receiving stand the dignitaries retained presence of mind only to locate a convenient chair before collapsing into sleep. The President was already dozing; he opened his mouth and emitted a few snorts indicative of deeper slumbers, while his lady slept decorously beside him. A stray seagull alighted on the Secretary of State, and went to sleep on one leg.

Close overhead, at what had been the center of the disturbance, floated Urizel, the woman he had rescued sleeping in his grasp. He spotted the stalled ambulance, which emanated images of physical aid.

"Wake up," he said to the crew. "Here is human hurt." They snapped back to consciousness rubbing their eyes, and jumped to man the stretcher.

"Put her here."

A press photographer beside them also woke, reaching by reflex for his camera, and got the banner headline shots of his life—Urizel stooping low with the unconscious woman draped photogenically across his tentacles, his great eye luminous with compassion and concern. "ALIEN RESCUES WOMAN FROM CROWD! ALIEN CARRYING GIRL HE SAVED TO AMBULANCE!"

(I found out from Kevin, who had been there too and waked first, that the photographer had luckily missed an even more sensational shot. Urizel, noting that this human he carried seemed to differ from the astronauts, had seized the opportunity to check out the locations and nature of those "lumps" Todd had told him of—in the process rearranging quite a lot of her clothes.)

The woman turned out to be a Mrs. C. P. Boynton. She was only slightly bruised, and her statements to the press were ecstatic.

"I was so scared, I knew that hundreds of people would trample on me and I'd be killed. I just prayed to God, 'Help me!' And suddenly there was this great blue being flying

over me like an angel, and he just reached down and pulled
me out from under all those terrible feet! And oh, he smells
so lovely!"

What I want to convey is that the Angli would be getting a
very good press, right from Day One.

Back at the stand, the official greetings to and by the
President finally came off. Perry tactfully roused the great
man by murmuring, "Sir, I believe you were about to say a
few words," and he automatically rose up into his speech—
just in time to divert the aged councilors from returning to
their ship. And the band began to play, rather disjointedly—
but it isn't true that they then or ever played "Nearer My
God to Thee." And the reception rolled off.

When it came time for Todd, Jim, and Perry to part company from their alien friends, with whom they'd spent over
a month of intimate travel, things got pretty emotional. During the voyage home, the Rev. Perry had been observed to
attach himself to Azazel in particular. Now, up on the receiving stand, the great blue forms of the Angli were turning
away, to go back to their ship and leave the humans to their
own. They were up on their back tentacles, their heads
towering above everything as they bade polite farewells to
the President, his lady, and the Secretary of State, now mi-
nus his seagull. Perry quietly moved closer. Suddenly he
dropped to his knees and flung his long arms around the
tentacles Azazel was standing on. (Perry was a huge man.)
After a moment of confusion, it became clear that he was
simply hugging the alien, his face laid against Azazel's side,
and weeping. He was also mumbling something that
sounded so private that no one listened, except Kevin. And
no one knew what thought-speech he was sending to his big
alien friend, or receiving back from him.

The strange tableau lasted only an instant. Then Perry got
up with great dignity and stepped back into line with Todd
and Jim. And the moment was swamped by the hand-tenta-
cle shaking going on all around.

Kevin, who had been just outside the stand, told me afterward that at the end Perry had said clearly, *"Non Angli sed*

angeli"—and if you don't place the quotation at first, listen on.

Now to sum up the impression the aliens were making, I'll give you a letter I received in response to my first appeal for eyewitnesses. It was written by one Cora-Lee Boomer, aged eighty-nine, like this:

"Of course I only saw it on TV you know. Maybe I saw it better that way. The Army cleared off this big sandy place, Dry Lake Something. And they had guards all over. But the people just filled it up. And about eleven A.M., I remember because it was time to feed the baby, Donald, we saw it coming down in the sky. It was like a big bunch of grapes only no stems.

"And it kept coming down, real slow, I guess not to hurt anything, and pretty soon a helicopter was going around it, taking pictures. It was kind of tan-colored, with antennae sticking out. All these round things pressed together like something I used to see—honeycombs. When they sent pictures from close up you could see all these blue eyes inside looking out. So beautiful. Excuse me, I can't say it right.

"Mostly I try not to think about it; even today I can just see it. But that man I had then, he thought he was so smart. And I was a young fool, I did whatever he wanted. He said that it was all no good. Stay away from Whitey junk, he said. Excuse me. I was so young.

"But when they landed and got out with the three men and I saw their eyes close up, I had a feeling he was wrong. They looked so beautiful. Like caring and understanding. And smiling too. I should have believed my own eyes.

"So I only saw things start. He came in and saw me looking at it and turned the set off—it was on all the channels, see—and said, 'Get my lunch,' So I never saw much of them after that. And of course I never got to go.

"I think now he was wrong, he was crazy. They were good, good. But I was so young and the baby kept me pretty busy, and with my job. Now I'm old I know there's more to life. I wonder what it be like. George, he's long gone.

"I just remember that big loving eye. Sometimes I cry a lot.

"I hope this is what you said you wanted. Sincerely, Cora Lee Boomer."

This is Theodora Tanton again, saying, well, that was the way the Earth's first meeting with the Angli went. I know the White Book doesn't tell about the riot, and the little points Kevin saw. But they're important, to show how people were starting to *feel* a certain way about the aliens, to explain part of what happened later.

People could have been disappointed, see, or bored. The aliens brought no hardware. And all the films and fiction we used to see kind of assumed that our first contact with ALIENS was going to result in a lot of new fancy technology, or at least a cure for the common cold. Goodies. But as Urizel said, these people brought us only peace and friendship—at least on the surface people could see. Their own goodies, like antigravity and telepathy, were just in their bodies— they could no more explain them or transmit them than we could hand over our sense of smell.

And then more things happened to excite the press. To everyone's surprise, the big ship simply broke up next day, with Angli flying pieces of it all over. Soon there was nothing left in NASA's guard ring but some struts and potted plants.

"ALIENS WANT TO SEE WORLD! ALIENS TO VISIT CATHEDRALS! ALIENS STUDY WORLD RELIGIONS! CALL FOR LANGUAGE-SPEAKERS! ALIENS DO NOT READ OR WRITE! ALIENS WANT TO MEET EVERY-BODY ON EARTH!" (That would be some of the youngsters chatting up the press. People had trouble sorting out the kids' stuff, at first.)

So Angli started turning up in little groups, or even alone, all over, at any time of day or night. Of course that gave the security forces of all the big nations total fits.

It turned out they needn't have worried too much about the Angli's safety. (Their own security was another matter.) But it's hard to assassinate a telepath—hostile thoughts blasted out signals to them long before the thinker could act.

I don't know if this is in the White Book or not, but just to show you:

One afternoon some Angli were in Libya, chatting with people at a market by a highway where cars were whizzing by like mad amongst the livestock and all. Suddenly every Angli grabbed a nearby human or two and shot straight up in the air, maybe twenty meters. At the same time, two more Angli grabbed a certain car, and flying with it, simply flipped it tail over into the empty space they'd made. Next second there was an explosion as a bomb went off inside the car, and a few people got cuts. The would-be bombers were dead.

It all happened so fast people were totally bewildered; they had to piece together afterward that some crazies had been going to blow the Angli up. And the Angli had taken defensive steps both for themselves and nearby people. That part of it was what stuck in people's minds when it was all over—that Angli automatically rescued you.

Then there was another big episode that may be in the White Book. It was when an Angli named Gavril was being taken on a scenic drive down the great road called the Corniche, in France. Gavril got tired of looking at the dirty Mediterranean—I guess he could hear the thoughts of dying fish and seabirds—and started casting about.

Next thing, he had flashed up onto the air from the open convertible, paced the car briefly, and then come to rest on a railway overpass. A rail line ran below the road. By the time his hosts got back to him, he was standing with closed eye, so evidently deep in concentration that they just waited.

Then train hootings began in the distance and Gavril opened his eye.

"Is o-kayee now," he said. "People see people." And he lofted back into the car, offering no explanation. Of course his hosts began questioning, especially as there seemed to be some excitement starting, down by the railroad.

What had happened, it transpired, is that Gavril had picked up the thoughts of two trainloads of people approaching each other at terrific speed in the tunnels below.

Happening to notice that the line was single track, he became concerned and hopped off to check.

Yes, he realized. They were heading for a frightful crash.
Gavril shot strong mental blasts at the trains' engineers—it
was hard work aiming simultaneously at targets speeding
opposite ways—*"Danger!* STOP!" As I said, it was difficult.
When he finally brought them to a stop, the headlight of
each train was just visible to the other.

Well, when his hosts realized what he'd done, they called
in the press, and hundreds of grateful passengers besieged
the scene. A photo of Gavril hovering over a locomotive,
captioned "ANGE DE MERCI," appeared in all the big French
papers that night. Apparently about six hundred people
would have died without his intervention; somebody, presumably terrorists, had buggered the automatic switch and
alarm systems.

Well, of course there was no holding the media after that,
and scads of episodes, true and concocted, were headlined.
There grew up a feeling that Angli were symbols of benevo-
lence or good fortune and that it was lucky to be in the
presence of one. People actually began plucking at them,
hoping to tear off a little scrap of "armor" to carry with them
like rabbit's feet, I guess. But of course they weren't wearing
armor; they were in their skins. The situation would have
been dangerous and painful had it not been for their telepathic warnings. As it was, a couple of youngsters got
scratched, and they all took to wearing flowing scarves they
could cut up and pass out. "Is a little cra-zee, people your
world," Todd said Urizel told him. Of course profuse apolo-
gies were extended by all authorities, but there is no control-
ling mobs. And the Angli began drawing *mobs*, crowds of
very emotionally wrought-up people, quite different from
merely curious or sensation-seekers.

During this period, there were things going on that I
should know and tell you, because for sure they're not in the
White Book, but you know, I never completed my research
—never began it really. To do so I've have had to go to
what's left of a dozen countries, and get into the U.S.S.R. and

even find certain hospitals. For the Angli were visiting places and talking to people they never saw fit to mention to NASA or anybody here, even to Todd, Jim, and Perry who had become their more or less official escorts.

Well, you may ask, what kind of inside story do I have, if I never did the research? Oh, the research was just an ornament I envisioned to the real tale that fell into my hands. Wait!

And that aside about the hospitals is a guess, by the way. It could have been university labs, or even private industry facilities. The gist of it is that somehow some Angli found the means to do a spot of sophisticated scientific research into human physiology. And they seemed to have an instinct for places where the press was strictly controlled, but that only came out later.

What came out then were two things of overpowering interest.

First was their plan to leave.

To leave? To *leave?* To just go jaunting off somewhere out in the galaxy—and maybe never come back?

This was a jolt. Maybe some higher-ups somewhere had done some serious thinking about how all this would end, but it hadn't reached the public. In fiction and films there was always some sort of permanence after the great Earth/Alien meeting; either the aliens were trying to take over, or Earthmen had beaten a path to their planetary doorstep, or *something* implied that there would be more contact, or at least some permanent effects. Not just this "Hello, nice-to-meet-you, bye-bye" business the aliens seemed to have in mind. A *visit*. Was that all this was?

The answer seemed to be Yes.

Why? Not that anyone had thought seriously of their staying around forever, but, well, why leave so *soon?*

Answer: They had things to attend to. There were all those beavers, or crocodiles, or whatever, sleeping up on the moon, waiting for the Angli to find them a water-world. And there were—God, there were all those *other* Angli up there, waiting to wake up when they found a real planet! And of course Earth wouldn't do. Here the Angli tried to be tactful, but it soon came out—Earth was to them a sort of planetary slum, too dirty and polluted and used up and overcrowded to live in. "An interesting place to *visit*, but—"

Not, of course, that any government had actually extended them an offer of real estate. (Some private citizens, especially those from Texas and Australia who seemed to own extraordinary amounts of the Earth's surface, did make some offers to "interested Angli families.")

What would be really nice, people thought, would be if the Angli were to settle on the Moon, or someplace relatively close. What about Venus or Mars? Couldn't they remake one, with some magical planet-shaping devices? And stay around?

Answer: Too bad, but we really haven't any magical planet-shaping tools, and everything else in your particular solar system is quite, quite uninhabitable. Sorry again.

As all this went on at an accelerating tempo, various people extended to the Angli some truly remarkable job offers, or suggested ways that they could make a living on Earth. Even the Mafia turned out to be very interested in their possibilities as security guards, with that telepathic alarm system. Strange Arabs called upon them at night. Several large churches even offered them substantial sums to stay and lead services. And a great many national intelligence or security agencies tendered offers.

All of these the Angli listened to with good-humored mystification. One evening when Earthly economics were being discussed, an Angli pulled out a coconut-sized pod filled with what appeared to be five- to ten-carat diamonds of exquisite color. "Like these good?" he asked. "We pick up, over there" —waving a tentacle in the general direction of the Alpha Centauri. "Go get quick." By the time the matter was explained the bottom had fallen out of the diamond market from Pretoria to Zurich. And it was intimated that they had resources of gold, or anything you cared to name, cached about.

What they really liked, personally, was flowers. Particularly dandelions of large size. Private applications to the Angli took on a distinctly different tone after this.

But it did not affect the public's emotional view of them as simply benevolent miracle workers, angels of mercy—or, now that we are getting nearer to the point, simply angels. Clearly a great outcry of mourning, a great weeping, lay ahead. The day they would leave would be so black. People couldn't think about it.

And then came the second event, or shock.

The Angli seemed to be completing their study of our cultures and especially our religions—if "study" isn't too formal a term for what they did, which was simply to ask questions. They were very interested in anything we were doing, whether it was running a paint factory or conducting a service in Notre-Dame. But they always asked people about their beliefs, or rather, about their god or gods. And one question which never failed to come up was, "Where is your god?"

After they had received an inventory of descriptions of, say, the Hindu pantheon, they always wound things up by asking, "Where are they? Where are they *now?*"

They got strange answers, of course. People pointed to the sky, or Westminster Abbey, or the Golden Pavilion; one man took them to the Grand Canyon. But when it came to *seeing* a given god or gods—well, we had to struggle with terms like "immaterial" or "transcendent" or "immanent." And they seemed . . . not exactly disappointed, but very serious.

Finally one day Todd turned the tables on them. "Do you have a god?" he asked.

"Oh yes. Many."

"And where are your gods?"

They were talking on a balcony overlooking the moonlit Great Pagoda of Moulmein. Azazel waved a tentacle moonward. "Up there."

"Your gods are up there with your ships? In spirit, you mean?"

"No. Gods—there! Many. Most medium, some very old, one new big one, the greatest now. In ship.

Well, everybody figured they were sculptures, or images, or sacred relics of some sort. But the Angli assured us they were alive, very much alive. Only sleeping, like the other Angli.

Well, uh, er . . . could they be seen? Could we go there and see some?

But they were asleep, Azazel repeated. Then he and Urizel conferred.

"Maybe is good they wake up one time," Urizel concluded. "Travel sleep long. You want we bring them here, show you?"

Did we!

Three reporters were present.

"ANGLI HAVE REAL GODS ASLEEP ON MOON."
"ANGLI GODS TO VISIT EARTH!"

And so an Angli delegation took off for Luna, to prepare their gods. And U.S. officialdom prepared to receive a supernatural visitation. Of course they didn't believe, then, that they'd be getting anything supernatural; their thinking ran to imagining Angli dressed up in costumes.

But the Angli seemed to be taking this very seriously. They returned from all over Earth, and their original ship reconstituted itself. Seeing this, the reception committee decided they had best take it more seriously too, and a committee of Earth's religious heads was convened to be in the reception stand. The Pope at that time was a great traveler, and very with-it; he insisted on being present. Of course, this threw official ecclesiastical circles into turmoil, as sanctioning a pagan religion. But he said, "Nonsense. All of us better come, to see what they've got." And the Patriarch of the Greek Orthodox faith for once agreed. The two British Archbishops were naturally eager. And the Protestant denominations joined in. So, seeing this unprecedently ecumenical gathering of Christians, the heads of other faiths were stimulated to attend, and what had started as a simple showing of alien idols, or something of the sort, grew into the full-scale worldwide summit meeting of every religious affiliation that we all saw on TV. It all required a special super-committee, and the protocol was a nightmare.

What it was really like, by the end of a few days, was a sort of confrontation of all Earth's religions with their alien counterparts. But it was a confrontation we'd lost from the start: while we had human officials in all kinds of fancy garb and ceremonial ways, they had—gods.

As we soon saw, when, that night a week or so later—it took place at night—another great bubble-ship came drifting moth-quiet into the searchlights' glare and settled into its cleared landing spot. (The officials had learned from the first fiasco; there was a carpeted path to the reception committee, but the whole area alongside the ship where informal Angli excursions might take place was cleared too. And the crowd was held well back, behind some temporary banks of seats to which admission was charged. Great video screens hung over the field, so all who came could see.)

And they came! The stands were soon overfull, with people crammed in everywhere.

As the ship settled, it could be seen that this was a larger craft, with bigger "bubbles," and a huge central bubble or dome. All the Angli were now present, lined up in a cordon around the perimeter in an unusually orderly fashion. And with them were a troop of Earth children, their arms full of flowers to present to the visiting divinities.

An outer door opened, and out shambled a huge, somewhat decrepit Angli figure, his great eye watering and blinking in the glare. He was festooned all over with what appeared to be animal remains, especially fish heads and tails, and his head bore the gigantic mask of some unknown beast.

"An—er—animist totem of early days," said the announcer's voice. "Surprisingly long-lived." Angli attendants handed the tribal godlet a dripping morsel to eat, and led it to a roped-off area of resting couches. It sprawled on tentacles rather than walking upright, being evidently from a time when the Angli were still semi-aquatic.

Next to emerge was a swathed barrel shape, obese and possibly somewhat senile. Its eye rolled in what appeared to be malevolent confusion, as it was led away waddling, leaving a wet, slimy trail.

"An early fertility deity," the announcer—a hastily summoned anthropologist—explained. "The next to appear will be avatars of this early form. You will note the increasing cultural complexity."

(The more alert members of the press, seeing the trend of events, were sending out emergency calls for anthropologists, ethnologists, and anyone who might interpret matters.)

"This," said one of these, as the file of ever-taller and more impressive Angli divinities made their various ways down the red carpet, "would represent about the Earthly level of Astarte or Ishtar."

The Angli goddess, a veiled form undulating past him, turned her huge eye and sent him a look that made him drop his notepad.

By this time it was evident, from the height and demeanor of the newcomers, that they were not ordinary Angli dressed in costumes, let alone statuary or mobile idols. No; this was another order of beings, coming into view before them in the night, and the crowd grew strangely silent. Even today, we don't know what they were. We only know we saw gods.

The last in this first group struck even Earthly eyes as a radiant figure, and she alone appeared conscious of the dignitaries' stand. The dazzling lights, her sparkling, shimmering form and veils, made her—for it was to all Earthly eyes a "she"—at one moment a bizarrely seductive alien, at the next a surpassing Earthly beauty. As she paced gracefully down the carpet, she flung up one cerulean limb, and out of the dark overhead a nighthawk dropped to it and perched there. From somewhere strange music played.

With a slight air of disdain she let her attendants turn her into the roped-off waiting area, and as she turned, her painted eye shot straight at the Papal Eminence an unmistakable wink. Then she stooped to accept an armful of flowers from a bedazzled child, proceeded into the reserved

area, and stretched out upon an oversized, scroll-ended di-
van.

It needed no commentator to tell the viewers that great
Aphrodite had passed by.

Behind her came a vast grizzled figure who limped, as had
the Earthly Vulcan. And after a little space, a towering,
commanding figure who glittered with menace as he strode
contemptuously down the way, alien weapons held high. Yet
his eye seemed clear and boyish, though all else spoke of war
and wrath; even so had Mars appeared to his mother.

Then came troops and bevies of bewilderingly decked
and jeweled figures, some carrying emblematic instruments
—minor deities, as they might be Muses, or Nereids, Oreads,
Dryads of the Greek pantheon, or Peris and Algerits and
Indus of others. These danced along under rainbows, piping
or singing, to herald the advent of a grand, hoary elder
figure, the inevitable old male of unlimited power and authority, whether Zeus, Jove, Wotan, or Jehovah. Although
the night was perfectly clear, the rumble of far-off thunder
accompanied them.

Singing had broken out among the Angli as they all passed
by; it was the first time humans had heard the Angli sing,
and they found the chants both strange and pleasing.

And on and on they came, deities resembling nothing
familiar to Western eyes but more familiar to Persian, Indian, or Chinese: some in weird built-out costumes and
serpentine decorations, great curled and feathered head-
pieces representing frowning grins, or elongations of the
eye to dreamlike proportions. In hieratic poses, they made
their ways to the appointed spot, and attendant heraldic
animals came with them. Also in the air were random
sparks, or flames, that looked sometimes like flowers, sometimes like snowflakes, but seemed to have a life of their own,
as they danced and clustered here and there.

Finally in the midst of what appeared to be a throng of
patriarchal tribal or national divinities, there stood out one
of seemingly great power, draped in long white robes. He
was oddly attended by what looked at first like small me-

chanical toys in the shapes of alien children, with sweet luminous eyes. But they were alive.

"A culminant patristic deity," the announcer explained. "He repeatedly reincarnated himself in his own son. Evidently he still has a few believers left. And now—" He went into a huddle with his Angli consultants.

In the pause that followed, all could see that one of the small son-figures had slowed to a stop, and seemed disoriented or ill. But a nearby Angli stooped and patted it solicitously, and it soon revived and ran on.

The somewhat shaken commentator was asking the Angli, "Why do you carry with you these—uh—apparently living gods of old dead religions? I'd think that your one real god or gods would be enough."

"Ah," said the Angli (some of whom could now speak several Earth languages quite well), "but you see, the minds and spirits of those who worshiped those gods are still in us, under the surface of civilization. And civilization can fail. When we notice that one of those old divinities is growing in vigor, in vitality, yes?—it gives us warning. Too many among us are unknowingly worshiping those qualities again. So"— he made stamping motions—"like small fires, we put out quick. You see? But now—"

The singing had fallen silent, and for a few breaths no one moved; there was a feeling of something impending.

Into the silence there stepped, or materialized, a tall robed and veiled figure twice the height of any that had gone before. It was indefinably female. As she came down the way, her face turned toward the dignitaries' stand, she gave no sign, but there was a concerted indrawing of breaths, almost a gasp. Across her single eye was a domino mask; in the depths of its opening could be seen a deep spark of smoldering red-gold. But where the rest of her face and head should be was only black emptiness under the hood. Her garments moved as though covering a gaunt figure, but no feet or hands revealed themselves. Where she passed, children hid their faces in their flowers. And the line of Angli bowed like willows in a silent wind.

Beside her paced an alien animal that she seemed to be restraining on a choke-chain; one of her long sleeves descended to its head, but no hand could be seen. Below the creature's eye was a tangle of tusks and cruel fangs; its limbs were coarsely padded and savagely spurred, and its expression was a blend of coldness and hate. Once, as she moved, her beast lifted its head and gave out a long-drawn baying sound, and the distant thunder growled.

As this apparition neared the stand, it was seen that a great single regal seat was placed for her apart from the others. In this she seated herself impassively. The surrounding Angli had dropped to what would have been a kneeling position in humans, and the nearby humans involuntarily turned their eyes away, and dropped their heads low.

"This is she whom we now worship," the Angli by the announcer said. "She has many names but only one essence. Here you might call her the Law of Cause and Effect."

"What is the . . . the animal?"

"That is her instrument of vengeance on all who violate her commandments. Either knowingly or unknowingly. Listen!"

From all around the horizon came the echo of a baying sound.

"Alas, my poor friends on your Earth—you do not worship her, but I fear your race has done violence to her Law. It may be that some terrible punishment is readying itself for you innocent ones."

Bravely, the human commentator asked, "You mean, like meddling with the atom?"

"No. That is just what I do not mean. That might have fretted only one of our tribal gods. The Law of Cause and Effect has no objection to inquiry, and she will always answer. Her vengeance is reserved for those who activate a Cause without desiring its Effect. Like the failure to anticipate the result of accelerated multiplication upon a finite surface."

"But—"

"Hush." To the crowds, who had heard little of this complex interchange and were becoming restless, he spoke out: "Please do not rise now. There is one more to pass."

But nothing visible came from the great ship. Only those nearest to it suddenly shivered, as though a cold wind had passed, though nothing stirred. It reached the stairs to the reception stand, and apparently flowed upward; several dignitaries were seen to hug their elbows to their sides and shudder.

Far away, lightning flashed, once. Then all was over.

"That was the shadow of the God to Come," the announcer said clearly. "Though what it will be we know no more than you . . ."

Did you see the Pope cross himself?

Well, the rest you must have seen; they took the ropes down and invited everyone who wanted to to mingle with the gods. (Luckily the security forces had been prepared for some such Angli-type informality, and got things organized in time.)

"In their present incarnate form, our gods are quite harmless," the announcer said. "But they do have a habit, when bored or restless, of dematerializing into pure energy—if I grasp your language correctly—and in that form they can be very dangerous indeed."

Even as he spoke, there came a high tinkling crash like expensive crystal breaking, from the direction of Aphrodite's couch, and it was seen that the goddess had vanished, leaving only a cloud of white particles like doves or long-finned white fishes, who danced in Brownian motion before dispersing.

A moment later the original old tribal animist deity also took himself out, with a minor boom, and the dancing of a few unidentifiable particles in the air where he had been.

But all this you have seen, and seen also the preparation of the Angli for immediate departure, after they took their refreshed gods back to Luna in the morning.

Their preparations also were highly informal, consisting merely of getting into their bubbles and reconstituting their ship with what souvenirs they had picked up. (They were partial to postcards of cathedrals and bathing beaches, and dried flowers.)

Aghast at the suddenness of all this, Earth prepared to mourn the departure of these wonderful visitors. And then the great announcement came. That you must remember. A senior Angli simply asked, "Anybody want come with us? We find good place."

Yes, they meant it. Would humans care to come a-roving with them? Not to be parted, but instead to find, with their dear new friends, a pristine Earth of clear sky and blue waters? A whole fresh start, with guardian angels?

Would they? WOULD THEY?

They would! —In such numbers that the Angli had to announce a limit of a million, to be accommodated asleep in their empty bubble-ships. There would be, by the way, no aging or death while in cold-sleep.

Their selection process, like everything else, was simple and informal. In the United States, Angli simply asked for room in parking lots (every shopping mall owner in the land offered one) and stationed themselves in any convenient place, holding a football-size pod that had an open end. Applicants were invited to hold one hand in the pod for a minute or two, while the Angli stared at it. The pod felt empty inside. Applicants could wiggle their fingers, hold still, or feel the sides; it seemed to make no difference, and the pod did not appear to change. After an instant or so the Angli simply said Yes or No, and that was that. Those accepted were told to go out to the ship with three kilos—6.6 pounds—of whatever they wanted. Suggested wear—this got printed on a slip—was one comfortable exercise suit, work-gloves, sun visor, and sneakers.

What basis were they chosen on, for this momentous voyage?

"They take the ones they like," Waefyel told me.

"But what does the pod do?"

"That way no arguments." I remembered these people were telepaths. An Angli could investigate a mind in depth while its owner was holding his hand in a pod.

But who is Waefyel?

Well, I forgot to tell you about meeting my own special Angli friend. Most of the rest of this comes from him. I met him, like so much else, through Kevin. Waefyel was acting as gofer for one of the aged councilors, who turned out to enjoy meeting humans at those big receptions. The aged councilor would run out of water, or that hard-tack stuff, which was all they ate, and Waefyel would get it for him. He met Kevin bringing coffee to a human counterpart.

Technically, Waefyel was a young adult, male (question mark—we *never* got that straightened out) and as nice as an Angli could be, which was very sweet indeed. But nice as he was, he couldn't get me accepted to go after I flunked the pod test. I tried again—they had no objection—and again and again, but it was always No—and then they were over their million.

"What's the matter with me, Waefyel?"

He shrugged, an impressive gesture in an octopus.

"Maybe know too much."

"*Me?* But don't you people like one to be smart?"

"No, *we* like. Only some kinds smart get killed by other humans."

"Oh." But I knew what he meant.

However, the Anglis didn't take a million boneheads, or a million anything. The group, what I saw of it when I went out to the ship, was as close to a random sample as you could come. (One selector *had* a weakness for redheads.) However, they did appear to eliminate obvious no-goods, junkies, the badly crippled—I tell you, *everybody* tried, before it was over!—and a lot of people I personally didn't like the looks of either.

The ones who got to go had a stamper pressed to their foreheads. It didn't leave any detectable mark, and they were told they could wash the place, or whatever. (That had to be printed too; the Angli got tired of answering.) At the ship, an Angli just glanced at the spot.

I asked Waefyel if it was a thought-imprint, and he laughed. "No need." I kicked myself mentally—of course, if a telepath looked there, the person's thoughts would automatically tell whether he'd been stamped or not.

Oh—one more thing about the selectees: At the ship, the men got misted with an aerosol and were given an injection.

"What's that for?"

Waefyel giggled.

"For fertility. You make too many young ones, no can educate."

"You mean they'll all be infertile? Won't they die out?"

"For twenty of your years only. Then another twenty. Then another." The concept in his mind was *cycle*. "Yes—that way no spoil everything, until learn better."

"How do they do it?"

And here's where I learned about the sophisticated research. Apparently some Angli who liked fussing with bioscience had found an opportunity to gene-splice a bacterium that would cause a human male's immune system to destroy, or rather inactivate, his own sperm. The antibodies, or whatever, wore out after about twenty years, thus allowing the man a couple of fertile ejaculations; but the system was self-renewing, and it kicked back in and the infertility closed down for another two decades. And so on. It was also dominant-inheritable.

Neat, no?

It seems there was an argument about the twenty years. Some Angli opted for forty, but they were persuaded that they were overreacting from revulsion at the state of our affairs.

And of course you know all about the rest.

I remarked to Waefyel, a pity they couldn't do it to all Earth. But the men's objections would be violent. He giggled again.

"You no see sunsets? Pretty green lights, no?"

"Well, yes, but they've been explaining that—"

"We do it already," he said. "Coming down in air now. Trouble, whew! To make so much. Good your bacteria breed fast too."

"What?"

Well, as I say, you know all about that. I was just the first to happen to know. Lord, I remember all the to-do, the fertility clinics besieged—of course it was blamed on women first. But finally it became too clear to ignore, especially as it affected a few related primates in a partial way. And the men had symptoms, too—they got sore and puffy when a large number of active sperm were getting killed.

But you know all that: how we have an oldest generation of mixed ages, like me and older, and after that one generation all aged about forty, and then another about twenty. And then nobody, but some women are just getting pregnant now. ("MOTHERHOOD AGAIN!" "HUMAN BIRTHS RESUME!" "WILL IT LAST THIS TIME?" It won't, I promise you.)

This was their going-away present to us, see.

"We do good thing you," as Waefyel put it. "Now maybe bad trouble coming not so bad."

And it hasn't, has it? We did just tiptoe by the worst of the war scares, but everyone worldwide was so preoccupied with trying to make babies that things quieted down fast. Of course it was hell on economies that were based on the asinine idea of endless growth, but that's a lot better than being exterminated. People who really go for the idea of a planet with fifty billion people standing on top of each other were disappointed. But all the ecological stuff, the poisoning and wastage and sewage and erosion, all became soluble, once the steady thunder of newborn humans cascading from ever-fertile bellies eased to a sprinkle every twenty years.

People would have had to face the idea of a static economy sooner or later; it was the Angli's gift to let us do it while there were still living oceans left.

But that's all beside the point.

When I got over the trauma of not being selected to go— no, I only *sound* like I'm crying—I was still worrying that little old question: Why, really, did the Angli leave that paradise planet they came from? *Why?*

"We want go see new places," Waefyel said. "We bored."

But he didn't say it right. Maybe telepaths transmit whether they want to or not.

"Waefyel—what *really* happened to those other people who were living on your planet?"

"They go away, maybe, or they die. I think they die."

That sounded sincere.

"Your people didn't kill them off, by any chance?"

"Oh no! *No!*"

You can't fake shock like that—I think.

"So you just left, bringing your gods with you. What about the Angli that are still there? What'll they do with no gods?"

"No Angli stay, is all here. Up on moon."

"Hmm. Small race, aren't you?"

"Three, four million. Is enough."

"And your gods. Hey, those gods were really *alive,* weren't they?"

We were lying on a little beach on one of the Virgin Islands, where Waefyel had flown us. (If only I could live on hardtack, what journeys we could have made! I did try the stuff, but it tasted like dried galoshes.)

"Of course they live," he said. "They do things for people. All gods do."

"Ours don't," I said lazily. "Hey, do other peoples have live gods?"

"Yes." His big eye looked sad. "Except you. You first we find. No live gods here."

"Hey, you mean it. I thought gods were just an idea."

"Oh no, is real. Look out, you getting too hot."

"Yeah, thanks. Why did your gods want to leave that lovely planet?"

"Go with us."

"You mean a god has to go where its people go? Hey, what happened to the other people's gods, the ones that died off? What happens to gods when their people die?"

"Usually—new word, see? Usually, gods go too. Lost in air, finish. Sometimes . . . not." His big eye was looking somber again. Not sad, just very serious. "We don't know why."

"Dead people's gods just evaporate. How sad. Hmm. But

sometimes not, eh? What happens to a bunch of gods who live on with no people?"

"I don't know." He sat up. "Look, is too hot for you here. I listen your skin burning."

"Sorry. I didn't mean to fry audibly." But I picked it up. What? Just something. Time to change the subject, for Waefyel. Well, maybe it bored him. But I didn't think it was that. In my bones, I felt I was poking into something hidden. Something the Angli wanted hidden.

"I hope your gods will like the new planet you find. You'll be there, with the humans, won't you?"

"Oh yes!" He smiled. "We find nice big one, lots of room. Lots of flowers." He touched a neck chain of dandelion flowers I had twisted for him. (Yes, they have dandelions and crabgrass even on the Virgin Islands.)

"I bet our people will go back to the stone age," I said idly. (I didn't care if they went back to the Paleocene, if only I could have gone with them.) "Hey, maybe they'll start worshiping that old totem-animal of yours."

"Maybe." As though involuntarily, his eye took on a dreamy smile.

"And then when they get more advanced, they can worship that Old Fertility Symbol. I guess they'll be in the mood. And work up to the lovelies. You know, that's neat! Here we don't have any gods of our own, and you provide us with a complete set, ready-to-go, carry-out gods! Why do you suppose we don't have gods of our own, Waefyel? Is something wrong with us? People *make* their gods, really, don't they?"

"I think so. Yes. What is wrong by you? We don't know. Maybe you have poison, maybe you kill gods!" He laughed and fussed at my hair—I had pretty hair then—with his tentacle tip. "But I don't think so. Some of the wise ones think you made a bad pattern of gods, some kind missing, see, so they couldn't go on and make more. A 'defective series,' that's right?"

"That's wrong, apparently. I wonder what we left out. Do you know?"

"No . . . but I think you got too many war gods. Not enough ones who take care."

"That sounds right." I was about falling asleep there in the beauty with the lapping little waves on the pink sand, and this lovely friend beside me. . . .

"I think we go inside now. Look Tee-Vee. I carry you."

"Oh, Waefyel." (Don't expect me to tell you about it, but we had something physical going between us. Especially then. It's not what you'd guess, either.)

Now there was a man staying at the hotel there. A serious older man, a sort of student. That evening we all got chatting, out on the terrace looking at the sunset. It *did* show the most lovely weird green light. Beautiful infertility, drifting down. The uproar about that hadn't started yet. Anyway, this older man started talking about angels. Rather pointedly, too. Funny topic, I thought.

"Did you know that angels were the lowest order of divine beings?" he asked me. "If there was something to be done, a flaming sword to be brandished, somebody to be admonished, or a message delivered—particularly a message—they called in an angel. They were the workhorses and message-bearers."

"Yes," said Waefyel unguardedly. I wondered what interest ancient myths about angels could possibly have for him. Probably he just enjoyed practicing his English; he did love that.

"Like gofers," I said. "The gofers of the gods."

So of course I had to explain gofers. (He *was* an older man.) Waefyel was delighted too. His first English pun, if that's what it is.

"How did angels get born?" I asked. "What about those little ones, cherubs, cherubim? Were they little angels?"

"No," said the man. "The connection of cherubs with infants is a late degradation. As to how angels got born, I wonder. I've never heard of an angel's mother or father."

"From the energy in the air," said Waefyel unexpectedly. "Elementals."

"Is there energy in the air?" I asked.

"You saw it. When gods dematerialize, a lot of it is around. Elementals," he repeated. And then suddenly frowned as if he were mad at himself, and shut up.

Next day we had to fly back. It was the twenty-third of August. The day after was the twenty-fourth. And even you must know what happened then:

They left.

Don't expect me to tell you a word about *that,* either.

Me just standing there, looking up at a vanishing point that reflected sunlight for one last instant. Me and a couple of million, no more than that—just standing there with eyes streaming our hearts out, looking up at a sky that would be empty forever. . . .

But at least I know, for all the good it does me, what had held me in its arms. Waefyel let out just enough so it had to be true. You get the picture, don't you? Or do I have to explain it?

I put it to Waefyel once, at the end.

"You're not an animal, like me, are you? You're something created out of energy, out of the minds of that race that died. You Angli are just pretending to be people."

"Smart little one."

"Like parasites. Oh, Waefyel!"

"No. Symbiotes—I know word. You good for us, we good for you."

"But you've trapped a million humans to go with you and keep you alive!"

"They need us. They happy."

Surely you see. There they were, when that other race who had made them died off—a whole complete pantheon-of-pantheons, all those gods from earliest to last, from highest to the lowest "workhorses." As good as dead, doomed to live forever on an empty planet with no living energy to need them or support them.

So what did they do? I mean, what did the higher-ups, the really big gods, do? This whole evolution of orphaned, unemployed gods, doomed with no people?

Why, they ordered their faithful workhorses, their lowest

order of functionaries, their *angeli* (the sound of that name was just one of those cosmic coincidences, by the way; it meant nothing to them)—well, they ordered their angeli to build ships and *take* them somewhere. To find a race that needed gods and take them there!

And eventually they got here and found a people with no gods. . . .

And now some of our people will have gods again. And the gods will have people. Let them; I'm not jealous. All I want is one of the gofers back.

My gofer of the gods.

People in the news business have long recognized something they call the Silly Season, a period of time when there's very little real news to report but the number of nutty items that cross their desks suddenly rises. People sit on flagpoles, swim upriver with the salmon, and see lots of "flying saucers." This story is about one such occurrence that's a Silly Season all by itself: a man takes out an ad promising to tell anyone the day he or she will die, for a substantial fee. And if he should prove he can do so . . . ?

Joel Richards's first novel, Pindharee, *was published last year.*

Mencken Stuff

by Joel Richards

I got to know Sonderman as only a jailer could.

Of course that was not the role I envisioned for myself when I first saw Sonderman. My first impression of him was the freeze-frame image, as I raised my eyes from the clutter of my desk, of a burly man, broad-shouldered and shambling, with thick curly hair and a heavy blond beard. Little skin showed from the neck up.

This was a freeze-frame of a man in motion. Sonderman was being taken through the newsroom to the office of the managing editor. His escort was Crane, head of the advertising department.

Sonderman had been very shrewd. His passage through the newsroom would have been more torturous if he had presented himself there first. He might not have made it at all. We have a screening process—a human filter, and I'm part of it—to weed out the crackpots. But Sonderman had not showed up at the newsroom reception desk with his story and a hope. He had approached the advertising department with hard cash in hand. Or the promise of it.

I hadn't paid much notice to Sonderman his first time

through. The return trip bore more the aspect of a parade. A many-legged dragon of a Chinese New Year parade, with Sonderman as its imposing head and a dwarfed Crane leading him on a flimsy tether. Filing behind were Crane's aide, Skorzeny, and Horvath, the managing editor. I gave this procession a more sustained scrutiny. Sonderman seemed composed and serene. Crane and Horvath, each an imperious ruler of his own fiefdom, traded wary glances, Crane having to do it over his shoulder. At least he had a backup in Skorzeny. Horvath, sensing a battle of numbers as well as ideas, stopped at the door and beckoned me to follow. I pushed back my chair, elbowed my way through the newsroom, and fell in at the rear.

Our destination was the publisher's office. Carroll T. Wainwright was used to receiving delegations—he preferred those conferring awards—and his office could handle a party caucus.

Also present, besides Sonderman and his entourage, was Jim—J. L. Tompkins. He had been in Wainwright's office and had been invited to stay. Or rather, no one, not even Wainwright, had presumed to invite him out.

Sonderman wasn't the most articulate of men. Perhaps he was, but had adopted a deliberately closemouthed bearing. He could write copy, though. He had written his own ad, which was now in Horvath's hand, via Crane. Horvath performed his conveyor belt function and dropped the sheet of copy on the publisher's desk. Tompkins walked around the desk and read over Wainwright's shoulder, bracing himself with one hand splayed on the desktop. Again, no one said him nay. Sonderman looked on benignly.

The ad made its case better than any verbal and less organized exposition could. It made it to all present, and to millions later. Here it is:

I CAN TELL YOU WHEN YOU'LL DIE
. . . IF YOU WANT TO KNOW.

You may not want to. But perhaps you'd want someone else to, so that they could arrange your affairs or buy life insurance to benefit your dependents.

Or you may want to know. Up to you.

I intend to prove this claim and to profit by it. A trust has been established with a major bank in this city as trustee. They are authorized to accept $10,000 from up to 200 respondents, these funds to be held by the bank in escrow. One month from this date I shall meet, individually and sequentially, with the 200 participants, clasping the hand of each for 30 seconds. I shall then write the date of each death on an index card and place the cards within sealed envelopes. I CANNOT PREDICT THE MANNER OF DEATH NOR GIVE ADVICE ON THE AVOIDANCE OF THESE DEATHS.

The cards and the money will be held by the bank in trust. When notice of the death of the first participant is presented to the bank, the trustee shall open the appropriate envelope and verify the date of death. If it is correct, the trustee shall deliver the remaining 199 envelopes to the participants and the money to the undersigned.

Note that there is a small measure of indeterminateness involved. All deaths occurring one year from date shall have a margin of error of one day from the predicted date. All deaths predicted within five years shall have a one week zone of prediction. Any deaths beyond five years shall be subject to a one month error factor.

Interested participants should respond to H. J. Sonderman, c/o this newspaper at the address below.

"This is bullshit," Tompkins said. He raised his eyes to meet Sonderman's challengingly. Sonderman met the gaze equably, and said nothing.

"There's obviously a great risk in running this ad," Wainwright said slowly. "Not legally. We can run a disclaimer as big as the ad itself. The risk is in looking like fools, or as accessories to a palpable hoax. No great newspaper can afford that."

That was probably the wrong tack to take. Our paper was not a New York paper, not a Washington paper, and not a great paper. It was a good regional paper, and had its moments and its awards. One of its major award winners was in fact present—Jim Tompkins, the H. L. Mencken of our day, said some; observer of the local *and* the national scene, and resident (and syndicated) debunker and curmudgeon.

"We can afford it," Tompkins stated. "But it's still bull-shit."

"I'm willing to pay five thousand dollars in ad costs to prove otherwise," Sonderman said mildly.

"That's something, J.L." Wainwright said. Tompkins winced. Wainwright believed, or wanted to believe, that Mencken stuff, and was always after Tompkins to use his initials in his byline. His middle name even started with L.! To Tompkins's credit, he had refused. He didn't tolerate bullshit from his publisher, either.

"Five thousand to make two million? Good odds. Why not buy a full page?"

"Because I don't have twenty thousand dollars, Mr. Tompkins," Sonderman replied. "I'm betting all I have in the world. That makes it a big-money bet for any man."

"We could run it—if we run it—as a full-page ad," Wainwright said carefully. "More effective, more impact that way. You could pay the rest in exclusive rights to your life story."

"No chance." Sonderman shook his bearded head decisively. "You can dig away—and you will, I've no doubt—but I'm not selling my life story. I'm selling something else."

Wainwright made a steeple of his hands and looked at Sonderman over them. "Suppose we're not buying, Mr. Sonderman."

"Then I try elsewhere. I live and work in this city. For the moment. You're the major paper here. And I don't mind Mr. Tompkins trying to prove my claims to be 'bullshit'—even retrospectively. May be an advantage, in fact. But if not here, I'll take it elsewhere."

"There would have to be safeguards," Horvath put in, as if it were decided. "We wouldn't want to be accessories to something worse—as if Sonderman hires a thug to gun down one of the participants during a robbery. On the day predicted, of course."

That created a stir.

"Interesting thought," Sonderman said when things had quieted down. "Of course I could stipulate that the remaining letters and the money be held until a second death is recorded."

"And that would double our culpability," Tompkins said. "Or triple it, if we carry it a step further. And you do, as well. And that's the only way I can see you making good your claim."

Silence held for a moment. That is, no voices were heard. Bodies shifted and chairs creaked.

"I have a suggestion," Sonderman said into the impasse. "Perhaps I could sequester myself, or be held in some type of informal house arrest, guarded by your personnel, for a couple of weeks preceding the first predicted death. Which date I'll know by then, of course. And the death can be autopsied for evidence of foul play. It's unlikely, of course, that it'll be anything but a natural body malfunction. Those are the odds, in fact."

There was a lot of backing and filling, with no one mentioning the main reason for our running such an ad. Not until the end, when it had been agreed.

"I still think it would be more effective as a full-page ad," Wainwright said.

"I oughtn't have to tell you your business," Sonderman said, doing so. "A quarter-page ad should do just fine. Black-border it and surround the copy with white space, if you like. Or run it across from your editorial page and editorialize on it. You'll get plenty of coverage—from other papers, lots of them. And you'll sell a lot of papers in the weeks that follow. And lots of ads in them, if Mr. Crane here knows *his* business."

Wainwright looked intently at Sonderman. "If I also didn't think you a fraud," he said, "I'd hire you."

In the next few weeks we learned a lot of things.

Not about Sonderman. We tried, though. Sonderman's trail went back about nine months—in this city, at least. Our earliest record of Sonderman's residence was at the waterfront YMCA. He had stayed there about three weeks, then had moved to the furnished studio apartment where he still lived. Within a few days of arrival in town—assuming he hadn't been in town under a different identity, which seemed possible but unlikely—he had taken a job as a busboy in a waterfront café. Shortly after, he had graduated to waiter. We gathered that this modest step up the ladder was obtainable by any busboy of a nonalcoholic and nontransient character—nontransient meaning not moving on within five days. A month later Sonderman had moved up to his present eminence of waiter at a distinctly better-grade eatery. One that called itself, and could actually make some claim to being, a bistro.

He must have lived a life of modest or no indulgences to save five thousand dollars, assuming that he had little with him when he blew into town. And yet—how could any reasonably intelligent man without entanglements *not* put together five thousand dollars if he had the time and the drive? Perhaps not, if he had recently been released from prison. As a con man, perhaps. That was the immediate assumption. Using informal channels we checked his fingerprints through the systems of the United States, Canada, and the United Kingdom. Not only did we turn up no criminal record—we turned up no record at all! No registration or service in any armed forces. Nothing.

Sonderman refused all answers. Was he coming off a bankruptcy under another name? No comment. Was he a citizen of another country? He had, in fact, a faint accent that we couldn't pinpoint; neither could an expert the paper hired. And yet the Social Security number that he used had been applied for nine months ago. Any comment? None.

And so on.

Then there was what we learned. Rather, what we decided on. First, we couldn't investigate Sonderman's work associates or other contacts too closely without the risk of arousing curiosity. Once we ran the ad, and even before, we didn't want to give the competing media a handle on Sonderman. And this was fine with him. He insisted on working up to and through the appearance of the ad. He needed the money, he said, perhaps not seriously. I suspect he also wanted to fill up his days. If ever a man embodied the concept of biding one's time, it was Sonderman.

Another thing we learned was that we didn't want the ad directing responses to the "undersigned." Not even to a fake name like Sonderman. The reasons were the same as those hampering our inquiries. So we changed the ad.

Meanwhile the legalities dragged on. We tried to keep it simple, but lawyers will be lawyers. It took a month to get the trust arrangements made, the documents drawn. That was lightning speed by legal standards. And then Sonderman temporized.

"What's the problem, Sonderman?" Tompkins asked with a touch of malice. "The moon phase not right? The goat entrails not coming up propitious?"

"Back off, Tompkins," Sonderman replied. "I have other reasons." Sonderman had a mild manner, as do many big men, but he didn't tolerate lack of respect. His attitude was: stay skeptical but don't address me as a fraud until you can prove it. In time Tompkins came to respect Sonderman and even like him. Tompkins did resemble Mencken in that one regard: he respected and enjoyed the company of politicians and other con men more than that of those they gulled.

"What are the reasons?"

"I'm a little short of my five thousand dollars. I'll have it earned in a week or two."

"Damn it—we'll waive the difference!" Wainwright exploded. "We're talking about what—hundreds of dollars?"

"Two hundred. And, no, you won't waive the difference. I intend to deliver a cashier's check for the full five thousand dollars to you, and I will."

In two weeks he did. On November 3, 1999, we ran the ad.

All hell broke loose. In the newspaper game we thought we knew the meaning and upper limits of that phrase. But we were wrong.

Disclaimer or no, most of the media treated us as almost a laughingstock. Not quite. No one wanted to risk having to eat crow, and all wanted a shot—through us—at Sonderman.

Sonderman cooperated in staying underground. He kept on waiting on tables. As he pointed out, he'd have to live in a large global village afterward, as a fraud or a man with fearsome powers. He intended to disappear with as much anonymity as he could muster. He was pretty good at anonymity. We hadn't learned any more about him, and none of our small circle could do more than guess how he'd look without that briar patch of a beard.

He continued working at his job up to the big day. Meanwhile, we'd certainly had no trouble getting takers. Wainwright had bought in, offering payment of the ad and five thousand dollars. Sonderman had laughed, pointing out that he'd already paid for the ad with five thousand that came tougher than Wainwright's ten. He particularly wanted his hard cash, and Wainwright ponied up. So did Tompkins, our ace debunker. There were plenty others as well, as we had to adopt a first-come-first-served priority, with the only qualifications (other than the ability to pay up front) being Sonderman's. He wanted at least sixty of the two hundred to be over sixty-five years old on the grounds that he wanted a death and his money fast. Reasonable, but cold-blooded.

While the business arrangements went on, the ballyhoo crescendoed. It included flak along with the skepticism. Religious animosity and downright threats from what we hoped were ineffectual crackpots. Death to the penetrators of God's mysteries. That sort.

It seemed like a long month, but it did come around. On the big day we convened at the world headquarters of the trustee bank. Security was most stringent. All entrants to the bank had to submit to X-ray and metal-detection search. We had planned other, more far-reaching measures as well.

Horvath had suggested that the two hundred participants be masked, and identified only by a number, that number to be later matched against a list of names—another measure to negate the possibility of Sonderman's effecting their deaths by some indirect means. Sonderman was quite agreeable. Surprisingly, the majority of the participants were not. They were pretty much a buccaneering type, or had once been. As one salty foreign-currency arbitrager put it: "Damn it, if he's going to call my death—and if I'm paying him to do it—I damn well want to look him in the eye. And I want him looking at my face. If he's a fraud, I want him to know the kind of man he's thinking of fleecing. Or killing."

Apparently one—or more—of the participants had seen that possibility, too.

So there we were. Sonderman was with me in an anteroom adjoining the room for the meetings, conferences, confrontations, whatever one chose to call them. He was as restrained as ever. Why did I choose to look upon *him* as the condemned man? At the door stood an armed security guard, and in the room through that door was a desk where sat a bank officer with a card index file and stacks of cards and envelopes. There was a comfortable chair for Sonderman, and adjoining it was a small table with a decanter of sherry. Though it was morning, Sonderman preferred a heavy cream sherry. There was only one glass; this was solitary drinking with a vengeance. Sonderman had made it clear that he'd speak not a word to anyone, nor socialize in any way. There'd hardly be time. At intervals of one minute, each participant would enter and walk over to Sonderman, who would rise and take his hand, holding the clasp for thirty seconds. The participant would leave through a second exit door. Sonderman would think his thoughts, make his notation and pass it to the trust officer, and sip his sherry.

For three hours and twenty minutes.

Sonderman looked at his watch, nodded to us, and entered the room.

Three hours and twenty minutes had gone by, and Sonderman was a different man.

He looked shaken. This in a man who had kept a calm imperturbability in the face of acerbic assaults from such masters of skepticism as Tompkins, and blunter assaults from those of lesser talent. Not to mention the religious fanatics and their threats. None had fazed him, at least to outward appearances.

Now he seemed exhausted and barely in control. Even Tompkins, that great diviner of bullshit, seemed subdued. No one pressed Sonderman now.

Sonderman slouched in that comfortable chair, looking not at all comfortable himself. One hand clasped his sherry glass, and the decanter was half empty. That much concentrated alcoholic sweetness would turn the stomach of any but a Bowery bum. Which maybe Sonderman had once been.

But despite the alcohol, Sonderman looked sicker of mind than stomach, ashen rather than ruddy.

And why not? If he indeed had the "gift" he claimed, it would be a strain to any man of minimal sensitivity to use it. Sonderman had looked death in the face two hundred times, with—to him—certainty. Sometimes, it was true, from a far remove of years. Or was ten or twenty years a fair distance to *whatever* Sonderman was? In some cases death must have sat immanently within the man or woman clasping his hand.

Two hundred times. Enough to shake any man.

Of course, Tompkins might have pointed out, facing that many men, some of great power and influence, whom you planned to swindle might do it, too. But Tompkins didn't make that point. I suspected that he was coming to respect Sonderman's divining ability or the consummate nature of his acting performance.

I was thinking of other things, of Sonderman's past. How often had Sonderman seen death in those he cared for? Or did he dare allow himself to get close to anyone?

Sonderman looked up from his glass and straightened up from his slouch. His gaze went directly to the desk calendar before him. It was the kind that displayed one day at a time in bold face, the kind that old movies showed flipping and fanning to denote the passage of time. The date today was December 5, 1999, a date of no particular significance. To us.

"You'd better lock me up," Sonderman said.

That's when I became Sonderman's jailer, or one of them. There were six of us, bachelors and reporters all. We divided the day into three eight-hour shifts, then broke the 4 P.M.-to-midnight shift into two four-hour "dog" watches. That ensured that no one was stuck with the same watch day after day. We got that "dogwatch" idea from one of us, Kassoway, who had been in the military.

Sonderman's furnished room was too Spartan—sleazy?—for any of us to stomach. Too small besides, and lacking in security. We moved Sonderman into a housekeeping suite at the Carleton. We could cook if we wanted, but had most of our meals sent up from room service.

As jails go it was pretty nice. Hell, even today's minimum-security prisons—which is where they stashed fraud specialists, such as Sonderman might prove to be—were a big step up from Sonderman's digs. So, tomorrow's millionaire or tomorrow's convicted felon, he had nowhere to go but up.

It was easy moving Sonderman in. Kassoway and I did it in a couple of hours. All he had was a few sets of clothes. We bought some more for him. It was cheaper than recycling what few he had through the expensive hotel valet service. And then there were the books. That was the bulk of what Sonderman moved in with him. Several suitcases and cardboard boxes of books.

While Kassoway and I wrestled the books to the cabinets, Sonderman moseyed around the suite. Apparently living quarters of more than one room were indeed a novelty. He looked into the closets, which his clothes hardly filled. He tried out several chairs. He investigated the wet bar and poured himself a bourbon and water. Then he padded back to the chair he apparently had selected as preeminent, and eased his plaid-shirted, bulky lumberjack frame into it.

Then he looked up at us expectantly. Expecting what?

Kassoway and I looked at each other and at Sonderman owlishly. He looked back. Then all of us burst out laughing.

After that it became routine. Tedious at times, for it was the holiday season and no one favored being cooped in, even in semiluxurious digs with room service to see to our needs at the paper's expense. Wainwright had tried to put parameters to the expense, or at least the time frame, since they were interlocked. Not long, Sonderman had told him. And Sonderman wouldn't say more.

We tried to make it as festive as could be. We had a small tree sent in, and we all took a turn at adding decorations. Tompkins visited now and then, and once he brought a present for Sonderman, quite gaily wrapped. Putting his finger aside of his nose and nodding to Sonderman, he carefully laid it under the tree. It turned out to be a signed copy of one of his several books, this one appropriately titled *Newspapermen and Other Con Artists.*

Tompkins liked to drop in and engage Sonderman in conversation, taking particular relish in Sonderman's increasing discomfiture. Sonderman seemed no longer imperturbable now that the denouement was near. He and Tompkins waged an undeclared and civilized skirmish over who—or what—Sonderman was. Tompkins was trying to get there on the broadest terms, questioning Sonderman on his interests, his knowledge, and the gaps in it so revealed. Some of the time Sonderman seemed to enjoy the diversion of these conversations while trying to reveal as little of himself as possible.

"I see that you're interested in cosmology," Tompkins would start out, after wandering the room and picking up a book on the latest in the Big Bang vs. blini/pancakes vs. null transferences. A popularization, but still not your bedtime light reading. "First causes are all very well. But how about teleology?"

"Teleology?" Sonderman questioned in puzzlement. "Last causes?"

"Certainly," Tompkins said, still pacing the room. "Onto-logical questions tickle the pure intellect, but I'm more interested in concrete human behavior. Teleology—the evaluation of conduct in relation to the ends it serves. There's something we can get our teeth into." He paused. "Your conduct, for example."

Sonderman laughed and shook his head. "Amazing. Cosmology isn't ontology, even if both deal with first causes. They're *different* first causes. And well you know it. The origins of the universe have nothing to do with explaining my conduct."

"And what does explain it?" Tompkins continued, not at all put off or put out at Sonderman's penetration of his specious logical two-stepping.

"My conduct is easily explainable, as are its ends. I'm acting so as to make money, and so that I don't have to go on waiting on tables all my life."

"And what will you do?"

"Other things besides wait on tables."

And so it went.

I guess it really wasn't that onerous, particularly when Tompkins was around to set off that kind of fireworks. We did have to stay alert so that Sonderman didn't attempt phoning out or otherwise influencing events on the outside. He never tried. I spent most of my time observing Sonderman and trying to draw conclusions. He read a lot, mostly metaphysical and philosophical works. You could call some of them religious—if you consider Zen a religion, for example, and some don't. He made notes in the margins, and I looked some of them over while Sonderman slept. Mostly minutiae or agreement or disagreement with the point at hand. Most were in English, but occasionally a foreign word intruded, as if Sonderman had another set of primary associations. I wrote these words down for future reference.

As counterpoint to these tomes, Sonderman had amassed a store of travel books and tour brochures. He spent a lot of time looking them over. He had quite cleverly collected literature on every continent, subcontinent, and archipelago known to man. While we could assume that he wouldn't hang around long if he collected—and he seemed to think he would—we couldn't tell what retreat he favored.

Soon Christmas was upon us. Sonderman didn't cheer up at these tidings. He seemed to withdraw into himself. Tompkins, who was also a bachelor, suggested a party for Christmas Eve. Sonderman agreed, it seemed with reservations. We soon found out why.

Everyone knows that Christmas isn't a merry occasion for many. I mean the chronic curmudgeons, the lonely, the very poor. None of us fitted these categories.

Still, the Christmas party was a fizzle. Four of the jailer/babysitters were present, drawn by the prospect of Tompkins's company rather than Sonderman's. Tompkins never showed. He called from the office to say that his father, who had long been ill, had taken a turn for the worse, and that Tompkins was flying cross country to see him.

We did our best, toasting each other with eggnogs and such, listening to holiday music, and swapping stories of big-city-newspaper peccadilloes and infighting.

At eleven the night man at the city desk called. There had been a major plane crash at the airport. He ordered the other three babysitters to the office, leaving me with Sonderman.

I kept my mouth shut till they had left. I turned to Sonderman. He looked ill.

I felt ill. And incipiently angry, too. Chilled. All of this together.

"Tompkins," I said.

"I don't know," Sonderman whispered hoarsely.

"Oh yes you do," I said, believing at last. "You son of a bitch!"

"Because I didn't wrestle the phone from you and tell Tompkins not to fly out?" Sonderman asked wearily. "Would he have listened? Would it have changed anything? It hasn't before."

I looked at him.

"I don't know *how* they die," Sonderman continued in that flat, tired voice. "Could have been a heart attack. You can't stop a man from taking a plane. Or a cab cross town. Or an elevator. Just because that *might* be it."

"Of course," I said evenly, "if Tompkins *wasn't* on that plane your prediction would fail, and he'd vilify you to your face and in print."

"That, too," Sonderman said. "But not for long, when the next on my list goes. But all this doesn't seem to matter. I can't change what will happen. I know." There was a look of tragedy, the personal sort, in his face. "I've tried."

"Then what's the point of all those ten-thousand-dollar-per-head customers purchasing your services if they can't change things? What of value do they get?"

"Foreknowledge," Sonderman said. "Or maybe nothing."

"Sonderman," I said, asking directly what Tompkins had been getting at in his circuitous way, *"what* are you?"

Sonderman looked up and visibly pulled himself together. I could see that old, defiant believe-me-or-be-damned look again. But now I believed.

"You're the investigative journalist," he said. "You figure it out."

Tompkins had been on the plane. His father had been ill, and for a long time, and had unexpectedly said he wanted to see his son. Tompkins's father knew what he was talking about. He died five days later without ever being told of his son's prior death.

Tompkins had gone to the airport without a reservation and had gone on standby. He ended up on the third plane out to New York, getting a seat at the very last moment.

The jetliner had collided on takeoff with a small private plane. There was no mechanical failure; it was controller error.

Tompkins's envelope at the bank bore the time of his death: December 24, 1999.

The trustee released Sonderman's two million dollars without hesitation and turned the remaining envelopes over to their new owners.

Sonderman had the money telexed to an already existing Swiss bank account. He also had a safe deposit box at a local bank which we had known nothing about, but learned of later. It contained what? A passport? Passports? Sonderman emptied it and bought a ticket to Zurich in his own name.

Of course we had a lot to ask him, not all in the nature of dispassionate journalism. As I've already indicated.

Sonderman was defiant now, and riding high. Ironically, only someone of Tompkins's irreverent, no-bullshit temperament might have faced him down and gotten answers. Sonderman told us, from me on up to the publisher, to screw off. Then he boarded that plane and left the country.

A week or so went by, and I did a lot of thinking. I kept my thoughts pretty much to myself. No one asked for them, anyway.

January is a pretty cold, cheerless month in the Midwest. No artificial holiday bonhomie remained, least of all at work. Tompkins was gone; the paper's best specimen of humanity and its ticket to immortality. His loss made the rest of us feel like mere workaday drudges, lost in reminiscence or railing in anger at the loss of a demigod.

A good time to get out. I had a month of vacation time accrued, and I planned to take it. I knew where. The question was when. There was one key piece in the puzzle still to be plugged in, and that fell into place on a Monday in early January.

It came in a letter to the bank trustee, copy to the paper. It came surface mail from Switzerland, taking two weeks to get here, though mailed the day Sonderman hit Europe. It was a safe bet that Sonderman was no longer among the gnomes, his money now in untraceable bearer bonds, perhaps even these turned over again. The Swiss *will* release information on banking transactions involved in crimes that are also a crime in Switzerland. Sonderman certainly knew that he qualified. Eminently.

Sonderman wrote that he was a fraud. Or genuine in a more limited way. His "gift," he explained, was in telling from a handshake when a person had less than a month to live. Then he could zero in with great accuracy. Beyond a month the permutations became ever more complex, interacting, and conditioned by outside happenings. At that remove his predictions were valueless. He had banked on one or more of the two hundred participants being due to die of natural causes—not at all dependent on extraneous events—within a month. He hadn't planned on Tompkins being the one. Anyway—it was all a swindle, but he cared enough to inform the participants so that they didn't structure their lives on the basis of phony predictions in those two hundred envelopes.

Interesting development, and it had everyone running around frothing at the mouth, trying to wipe egg off the face, backbiting, or laughing at the discomfiture of others. Depended on where you were in the hierarchy, and how instrumental you had been in promoting the Sonderman scam to prominence.

In all the turmoil, no one thought to question this new, revised account of Sonderman's. I did. As he had suggested, I had done some limited investigating. There were certain things I *did* believe about Sonderman. Not his original story. Not this version either.

I took my vacation and booked a flight for Lisbon.

Dateline Estoril. I'm sitting at an open-air snack bar by the beach, watching the play of color on the hills. Mimosa, plumbago, hibiscus, and some I don't know. It's shady here, a good place to while away the hottest hours while the sun does its hardest work and practically no one else does any. As good a place as any to run across Sonderman.

Sure, Sonderman may prefer a more scholarly milieu later. He is a scholar of some sort, I'm certain, and a proven bibliophile. But now I figure he'll want to treat himself to a little luxury while he winds down. As do I.

I want to talk to Sonderman. No direct confrontation on my turf, which he'd find threatening. I want a slow, desultory hour or two in a shady restaurant such as this. He can order for me. *Lagosta,* perhaps, with a cold Sagres beer. Or those strange shellfish—barnacles, I'm told—*ameijoas.* I can't wrap my tongue around that pronunciation, but I'm sure he can. Barnacles would be an adventurous choice for me, but maybe not for him.

Afterward we can switch to *vinho verde* and I can ask him things, very low key. How does it feel to be marooned in the past? Perhaps if he's sufficiently at ease he can tell me how it came to be. Did his machine—did he use a machine?—break down? Was he the first to do it? How come no one missed him and could rescue him? Didn't they have procedures for that? Or was this era proscribed? Was he a fugitive?

And all things like that. On a larger scale—what was the future like?

I'm sure Sonderman had little practical to tell me. He was clearly a man of arts or letters, with no scientific knowledge that he could trade on. Perhaps he could recite some future bard's poem of Yeatsian or Shakespearean caliber to astound and delight me.

A man of arts or letters. He had one pathetic piece of trivia to sell—the foreknowledge of the death of our preeminent social commentator and journalist on a memorable date. And give him credit: he devised a way to capitalize on this historical footnote, and to do it big.

It must have been tough to do it. All bullshit aside, I'll bet he *could* have kept Tompkins off that plane. In this timeline at least. After I've learned what I want to know, I intend to front him on this.

Estoril. Just one of the many travel brochures that Sonderman kept around for misdirection or future use. Sonderman's whole scheme and its embellishments were a masterpiece of misdirection.

Still, this isn't quite a needle-in-a-haystack search.

Sonderman's scholarly books. Among his English annotations he had penciled in an occasional foreign word. Portuguese.

Was that part of Sonderman's field of study, or was Portuguese the language of the future? Brazil as a world power—why not? And, if Sonderman doesn't show here, perhaps next vacation I'll try the universities and beaches of Brazil. A much larger task, many more people to sieve. But pleasant surroundings.

Next year—dateline Rio.

Herewith, a tale of a far planet that's beautiful and colorful. But the human colonists can be very ugly at times.

Marta Randall's novels include A City in the North *and* Journey. *She is a Past President of the Science Fiction Writers of America.*

LAPIDARY NIGHTS

by Marta Randall

The noise woke me; I lay in bed, listening to the bright sound of leaf on leaf. Another lapidary night, cracking leaves in the forest around the house. I thought dreamily of rising and walking into it, to fix the newly formed crystals before they shattered, perhaps to become crystalline myself. Instead I burrowed deeper into the bedclothes, listening to the rising wind. In the morning shards of emerald lay on the deeper emerald of the grass, or pierced the faceted violets. Another extravagance of jewels, littering my small clearing. I stirred them with one slippered foot, admiring their fire. Useless for my purposes, of course. Hawkins paid for perfection only: the unblemished beryl rose, the symmetrical ruby anemone, the pure silver tracery of veins through an emerald leaf. Or insects: moths, spiders, butterflies so delicate that too often they shattered in the collecting. Two years ago I found something that looked like a squirrel, russet, auburn, bronze and amber; black jet eyes bright and peering, the glory of a tail caught ruffled and raised. Hawkins took it eagerly and appeared the next week with a cage full of cats —scarce commodities on Suledan. I refused them. A squirrel caught in a crystal night is one thing, but I won't deliberately expose an animal. My adamantine goddess was not pleased.

After breakfast I swept broken leaves into the shallow moat surrounding the cabin. They clung to my broom, melting in the sunlight; in the dankness of the moat their colors mingled to a uniform muddy gray. A process of rot, Hawkins had explained: when things ripen on Suledan, their cells crystallize overnight, except for the seeds. The sun's warmth melts the crystals to provide both organic nutrients for the untouched seeds, and the gases that keep the new growth safe until it, too, is ripe for crystallization. The process interested me less than the result: the transfiguration of light, the translation of the mundane into the fantastic. A poet's dream, this glory out of putrefaction, and to preserve the dream I left leaf and grass emeralds lying in the shade of trees, where they would, with luck, flash and sparkle a few days longer. I put the broom away, gathered my specimen boxes, and went into the forest.

Nature thrives on curls and imperfections, the nibbles of insects and the vagaries of the sun, but Hawkins paid for perfection only. Originally I thought her an idealist, searching always for the pure, the unsullied, but I changed my mind. She had no sense of the beautiful, beautiful as she was; her taste ran to the brightly colored usual, devoid of imagination. During the first year, when pleasing her was a less vital and more romantic concern, I tried collecting fresh flowers and placing them where I thought crystals would form, but too many blossoms scorched to ebony. Now I simply walked the forest searching for the glorified mundane, and found clusters of perfect leaves, a spray of evergreen needles, two sapphire eggs in an abandoned nest, moonstone morning glories. The morning glories were no more morning glories than were the agates agates or the roses roses, but Suledan had no sapient indigenes to contradict my naming and I didn't care what the Suledano colonists called these plants, or how scientists defined these peculiar gems.

In the odoriferous dimness of my one-room cabin, I mixed chemicals and slid the specimens into the fixing bath. Hawkins's invention, that clear and viscous solution. I asked her once if untreated specimens still lived, caught in gems, before they melted. She shrugged the question away, uninterested in the minor moralities of life and death. I set an amethyst insect in the sun and saw a final spasm before it liquefied, but could not tell if I saw its death, or simply an angularity of the crystal. Perhaps, I thought, life did persist, and when I treated the specimens I gave them immortality. A pretty conceit, which I didn't share with the crystal bitch, who is not one for pretty conceits. I lifted my specimens from the bath, set them aside to dry, and pried up the loose board in the floor.

Hawkins appreciated gaudy perfection, but I didn't. My hidden stash glowed with the understated: opalescent, burnished, lambent, strange. After a moment's consideration, I added four leaves and one sapphire egg from that day's scavenging and knelt for a moment, considering my escape fund that someday, with luck, would buy my passage off Suledan. Two years ago, fare to the nearest grabstation came to two thousand Federation fremarks, or about three thousand of the local suldans. Two years of Hawkins's miserly commissions added to twenty-two hundred fifty suldans and the proceeds from my private hoard, the specimens I had hidden from Hawkins's greed, might eventually make up the difference.

I replaced the board and put the remaining gems with the other specimens in the transport case. They made an impressive display; I wondered how much Hawkins would pay me for them, then put the wondering aside. What Hawkins offered, I had to take. I rechecked my cupboard. Still a week's supply of food left, but Hawkins would be back soon. Terrans can't eat Suledano vegetation or meats—they're not poisonous, just entirely non-nutritious. I spent the rest of the day watching the sun turn emeralds to sludge beneath the neighboring trees.

Hawkins came the next morning, heralded by the shattering of grass under the hopper's air cushion. I watched her dark-robed figure descend from the hopper and turned away before she turned toward me; all the poetry disappeared, replaced by clammy hands, sweat, pounding heart —I catalogued the symptoms, but it didn't help. She dumped a supply bag beside the opened transport case and made a pleased noise, rotating a diamond moth between her slim fingers; rainbows fractured against my walls. Her robes reeked, as always, of rotting crystals. I watched her hands—safe, I thought, if I didn't look at her face, didn't see the color of her eyes.

"Find more animals," she said, her voice deep and smooth. "You should look harder—trap some, set them out."

Azure fingernails tapped the case. I shook my head. "No. How much for these?"

"Thirty-five." She bent toward the table, her robe clinging momentarily to the curve of her hips. I looked away.

"Last month you gave me forty—for a smaller group. Not as good, either."

"That was last month," Hawkins said, replacing the moth in the case. "Food's expensive, kid. And I'm taking the risks, not you." She closed the case and tapped the locks carefully before sliding the case into her saddlebag. "You give me more animals, then we'll discuss more money."

I shook my head. "I want fifty for this batch. It's worth it."

"You find animals, then maybe it'll be worth it. Or maybe you don't want the job anymore." Her voice richened; she always enjoyed this part. "Maybe you'd be more comfortable back in town."

I almost looked up then, and she laughed.

"Kid," she said genially, "they still got your picture up in the center of town. And all the Suledano schoolkids get marched by it twice a day so they can spit on you." One hip braced against the table, long fingers caressing the saddlebags, the pale skin of her wrist. I looked away, saw my messy, narrow bed, turned away from that, too.

"You used to be grateful, spacer," she continued. "I kind of miss that. You want to hear again what they do to murderers? They're real old-fashioned on Suledan—they like ropes. And knives."

"Damn it—" I said to the wall.

"And everyone comes to watch, too. Like a big party." I could hear her smile. A little silence grew—this was where she usually laughed, and said I was too important to her; this was where she sometimes, not too often anymore but sometimes, moved toward the bed. Instead she said, "I could tell them where you are, kid. I could turn you in."

I jerked around to look at her. Sapphire eyes today, above high ivory cheekbones, framed in curling amethyst hair—last month her eyes had been lavender jade, her hair silver and ebony. I lost my breath and she laughed again.

"You can't," I whispered. "You turn me in and you'll be—"

"Hey, I'm clean," Hawkins said, tossing the saddlebags over her shoulder. Her voice lost its honey, now that she'd won the game. "I spotted you in the forest, made a report like any good citizen. Found a fugitive murderer violating the export laws—they'll give me a goddamn medal. And my brokers aren't going to rat on me."

I couldn't talk. Smiling, she reached toward my cheek and I leaped back; Hawkins laughed again and dropped a bound packet of suldans on the table, mounted the hopper, and powered off, leaving me alone in the crystal forest.

She wouldn't do it. Would she? I paced the forest, fighting panic. Pale skin smooth against the skin of my thighs, curls spilling over my pillow (she rode above me once, agate eyes, her hair an azure waterfall between our faces and the world) —perhaps she'd found someone new, some other spacer in trouble. Gems flickered in the deep shade. She hadn't let me touch her in months. She wouldn't turn me in. Would she?

No. She needed me. A mantra against the darkness of the night: she needed me. This new threat was just another twist in Hawkins's game, and I could live with it, as I had learned to live with the others. She needed me. Fear and hatred and uncertainty—she needed me.

I cherished the thought, returning through the forest, crossing the shallow moat, upending the supply bag she'd left on my table. A flour sack filled with dirt, dinner pouches stuffed with sawdust, shards of rotting crystals in the drink sacks. She needed me? I ripped the containers apart, tore at the supply bag, emptied the rotting crystals of the drink sacks into the rotting crystals of the moat. The final twist to her game, of course: that I could choose starvation in the forest or execution in the town. I gripped the edge of the table, terrified of my own rage, and slowed, and stopped, and breathed until my breathing steadied. Hawkins won, Hawkins always won, but not this time. I would not die. I would not give the bitch the satisfaction.

The makeshift backpack from behind the pile of my clothes. My remaining food, my remaining water. The pile of suldans, an empty specimen case. Crystals gleamed when I tore aside the loose board; they warmed my hands as I lifted and nested them, one by one, in the extinguishing darkness of the case. I wrapped the case in a dark robe, the one Hawkins gave me when she smuggled me out of town, and fitted everything into the backpack. By early afternoon I was walking toward town, avoiding the barely discernible route Hawkins always took, following the stench of rotting crystals.

Neat as parkland, the Suledan forest has no deadwood, no thickets of brush; Suledan holds neither oil nor fossils. The trees lose leaves and bark to the crystal, leaving smooth, pale heartwood, and when I roamed the forest, I looked for dark and shaggy trunks amid the vines and long-limbed flowers. Now I followed naked boles and thick scent, working my way east. In late afternoon I passed through a glade on the verge of crystallization; in the evening I found a rotted spot to spend the night. Nearby, a stream sang.

The settlement lay in a broad river valley, surrounded by a kilometer of scorched earth; roofs and covered streets created a hodgepodge of protection against the sun. Suledanos lived in perpetual shade, decked in covering robes, sprayed daily with the essence of rotting crystals, terrified of their world. I cursed them and skirted the town, moving toward the port.

It, too, hadn't changed: a pale expanse of setdown, the dingy one-story terminal, the clutter of hovercars and battered cargo vans, the scent of lubricant. It smelled like heaven; some spacers claimed to hate it, but Suledan had been my first trip, and that thick, sharp odor made me want to cry. That and the growl of an approaching shuttle, soon followed by the gleam and flash and deeper roar of setdown.

I crept across desolation, finding a place to hide amid the cargo vans. An hour later the crew spilled into port sector, shouting and laughing and flinging their arms wide, while I scurried after. In two years I'd seen only Hawkins's mutable face, and my reflection in the facets of jewels. I tried not to stare. They must have thought me a local kid, tagging along in worshipful adulation; the kid I'd been three years before. A few laughed and held their noses against my stink; the others ignored me. Hidden in their roistering, I walked toward the center of the sector.

Spacers glitter and flash, decked in eccentric layers of color, blazoned with web scars, but the Suledanos are a dour sort, dark and grim. A number of them risked the open streets in port sector, faces buried in their hoods, fastidiously holding their robes away from the spacers' gaudiness. I held my breath, but they glared at me no more than at the others. The spacers stopped to argue about bars and whorehouses and where to spend their three days' leave. Over their shoulders, I saw the sign for Spacer's Haven, and I backed away from the group, turned, walked off. I had killed a man in Spacer's Haven.

Ahead, the vivid, sunny street slid under the overhanging roofs of the colony; I walked toward the dimness, peering in shop windows. The clutter of a fitter's, a café promising off-world delicacies and reeking of grease, a couple of whores lounging against the dirty window of a vid parlor. They called to me amid the constant, startling roar of the sector, and when I ignored them they cursed me for a baby. Eventually I found what I wanted: a shop settled modestly between the sunlight and the shade, sporting a discreet display of jeweled leaves and a brokerage sign. I had picked those leaves the day before. I put my hand through the shimmer of the door and went in.

A single chime, the scent of fresh apples, thick amber rugs, specimens bedded in velvet behind vibraglass. The woman behind the counter, decorative as her merchandise, looked up from her book, clicked it off, and rose.

"Good morning," she said amiably, looking at my stained clothes. "May I help you?" One glittering eyebrow rose.

"I don't want—I mean, this is a brokerage too, isn't it?" I waited for her nod, my palms damp. "I've got something to sell." I shrugged out of my pack, but she put one hand up, forestalling me. Tattoos shimmered along her fingers.

"Our merchandise is specialized," she said, still amiable. "There's a fine pawnshop—"

"I don't need—. Can you just look at what I've got? Roses, butterflies—"

"We *don't* deal in illegal exports," she said sharply. "Perhaps you're new on-planet. Suledano law prohibits export of native flora or fauna. In any state."

I stared from her to the elegant jeweled pinflowers in the case.

"Handcrafted," she said. "A local art."

I shook my head, then realized her problem and pushed my sleeve back.

"Look, lady. Here's my license; I'm a drive-jock, not a knocker, or a cop. I don't care what the laws are—I've just got some stuff I want to sell. Okay?"

She inspected the license embedded under the skin of my forearm. "These can be forged," she said, but she was smiling.

"The hell they can. You want to see what I've got?" I reached into the pack for the specimen case.

"God's love, spacer, not in here," she said quickly. She came around the counter and palmed the shop door; the shimmering opaqued. "Come into the back. Well, come on." Black velvet draped the doorway; she held it aside and I followed her into a small room. Shelves, racks, an orderly clutter. High-intensity lamps flickered and glowed as she walked around a square table; jeweler's loupes glittered.

"You have some trinkets?" she said as I pulled out the specimen case. A corner of her mouth curved up, and I knew what she expected. Dumb spacer picks jewels in the forest and, when he tries to sell them, discovers they've turned to sludge. Then she'd have a good laugh and kick me out. "You're not the first spacer to run short of funds and make a trip to the forest," she said as I flicked open the catch on the case. "But I should warn you, most of the stuff you pick up isn't worth . . ." Then she ran out of words and stared.

I stepped back, watching her. After a moment, she picked out a sapphire egg and peered at it through a loupe. Good choice—the denser specimens were often imperfect, but this one was flawless. An aquamarine bird, lapis lazuli snakes twined together, a small furry thing with ivory tusks; one by one she inspected my horde, and when she finished she stood back and looked at me.

"You're Hawkins's scoop," she said. "Wait, don't leave. I won't tell her."

I stopped halfway to the door and looked at her. She put her hands flat on the table.

"Once a month Hawkins disappears for half a day, comes back with dozens of perfect specimens, and nobody knows how she does it. We figured she must have help. Do you have a name?"

"Does it matter?"

She shrugged. "Not really." Her mouth curved again. "What does she pay you, spacer? Money? Sex? Or both?"

I put my shoulders back. "Do you want this stuff?"

"Of course. I'll even pay you what it's worth, which is probably more than Hawkins does." She touched an embedded keyboard while numbers flashed and danced along the table top. "Nine hundred seventy suldans; that's fifty percent of what I'll get for them. Have we got a deal?"

"Can you pay me in fremarks?"

She nodded, counted out six hundred forty-seven fremarks, and banded them into a small, neat package.

"I'll take any specimens you can find," she said. "Of this quality. Laila Sa'ad—remember me. But for God's sake don't tell Hawkins—she'd kill for less." She glanced at me. "I mean that."

I slid into the backpack, put the fremarks in my pocket, put my hand on top of them, and nodded and smiled and left, clutching my freedom. It took all my will power not to run down the bright street to the port. The setdown shivered with heat; the factor's office was dusty and close. He yawned and checked his database, ran a flat finger down the screen, and announced, yawning again, that there was room on *Skiffle,* departing in three days. Lower level only, payment in advance. I dug into my pocket while he cleared me through the Federation roster, and when he turned back I had the money stacked neatly, fremarks on the left, suldans on the right. He frowned at the suldans.

"Any problem with mixed currency?" I asked, knowing that there wasn't.

"This currency ain't mixed," he said slowly, flicking the suldans with one broad fingernail. They fanned over the counter, red and blue and white. "This ain't currency."

I stared at him. "Of course it's currency, it's suldans, it's my pay—"

"It's junk. There's no paper money on this planet, kid. This ain't even counterfeit, it's new New Edo yen, and New Edo went bankrupt forty years ago." He grinned suddenly. "Somebody paid you with this? And you took it?"

For a moment I couldn't breathe. The factor giggled and fingered his 'base.

"Wait! I've still got the fremarks, six hundred forty-seven; can I buy passage in stasis?"

"Ship ain't equipped." He looked at my suldans and giggled again.

"I'll work. Any berths open? I'm licensed." I pushed back my sleeve to show him.

He played with his 'base again. "Naw. Didn't think so. Nobody jumps ship on this place."

"Okay, hold it, when's the next ship due? Maybe I can wait. . . ."

The factor shook his head. "Three months. Give it up, kid." He flicked the 'base off and went back to his office. "Hey," he called over his shoulder. "Get that garbage off my desk." The door snapped shut behind him.

My hands shook so hard it took three tries before I could

gather the fake suldans; when I went outside they slid through my fingers, scattering across the setdown. Hawkins. I had been on planet only a few hours before the fight, before she hustled me into the forest. Stupid kid, stupid spacer—God, she must have laughed at me. I stared at the bright New Edo yen, flipping and dancing in the spaceport breeze; mechanics swarmed over the shuttle nearby, voices harsh, tools banging and clattering and loud. Stowaways are deep-spaced; it's Federation law. Suledanos kill murderers with ropes and knives, and everyone comes to watch. Hawkins left me in the forest with a bag of sawdust and a bag of dirt.

The breeze tweaked my hair. I felt suddenly naked, bare to sky and fate and Suledano schoolkids. I took the cloak from my backpack and put it on, hid my face, walked away from the port. My stomach hurt. Hawkins liked to see me crawl. Maybe she'd take me back. If I begged. If only for entertainment's sake. She'd take me back, and I'd scour the crystal forest, build my collection again, bring it to Laila Sa'ad. Maybe six more months, if I worked hard. Maybe a year. What choice did I have? The hood hid everything save the patch of street before me, and the whores left me alone.

Hawkins wasn't hard to find. The public directory gave me her address; after half an hour of wandering the maze of covered streets, I rounded the corner of a mansion and froze.

Street lights, door lights, floodlights, ground lights; the glare bathed a large hovervan and movers loading passage boxes. The boxes sported Federation intercargo insignia. Hawkins watched from a second-floor balcony, white silk, quartz eyes, leaning to point an ivory fingertip at the leader, a tall woman in spacer's gaudy rags. I ducked back, heart pounding. Honeyed voice, servile response, grunts and clatter, a lift field whined. The bitch was leaving me. To starve in the forest, she thought—if she thought of me at all. Getting out clean. I risked another glance. Hawkins was gone; the leader consulted her flipboard and the movers worked rapidly, the skirts of their robes tucked up between their legs, hoods pushed back. One glanced my way and I ducked my head, walked away with hands clenched in my pockets, trying to imitate a Suledano's dour gait. It was very hard to breathe.

Spacer's Haven had a raised dance floor, circled closely by tables. The bar looked smaller, darker, dirtier, eerily quiet. A Suledano lurked behind the bar; the bartray brought me a kravath, took a fremark, dropped Suledano change on the table, floated away. I fingered the coins as I drank: milled edges, the planet's name on one side, the denomination on the other. Plain, ugly coins, but they bought me three more glasses of kravath. I lined them up on the table and downed them in order, staring at the dance floor. That was where it had happened, on the side farthest from the door: drunk and happy, seventeen, dancing with another spacer until one of us tripped and we spun around each other, trying to find our balance. We fell into a table of locals; one screamed and jumped for my throat; I grabbed his shoulders; the table collapsed around us. I sat up, still laughing, still ready to fight, but the Suledano lay still. Everyone was yelling and swinging, and a woman with opaline eyes grabbed my arm and rushed me out. And nothing marked it, save that I was here again, and drunk again, and there was no way out. The crystal bitch, Suledano law, wandering into the forest to become my own monument—it should have ended two years ago, before I knew, before I had a choice.

I suppose I said all this, loudly, because the Suledano barkeep came over and I tried to hit him, then threw the empty vibraglasses at the dance floor. The first one winked out halfway there; the last one, still full, left a trail of kravath behind it. Two chairs followed it, but the bouncer got to me before I could lift the table. I tried to explain to it, trap and snare, circularity, but it tackled me, slapped a sobor on my arm, and called the port cops, while the barkeep howled curses from beneath a table.

Within an hour I was sitting in the port guardstation, frozen in a holdfield, sober. The cop took a print from my license and ran a data check on me, and I thought about ropes and knives, about the cabin in the forest, the marks of Hawkins's hopper on shattered grass, New Edo yen dancing in the spaceport breeze, all the details that bound us together. I could take her with me. Maybe they'd let me watch her die before I died—

When the cop released the field I looked at her, and smiled, and waited for it to begin. She frowned.

"You goddamned kids have any idea how much trouble you can get into?" she demanded. "Think you're under Federation law, but you assault a local and they press it, you go into local court, local law, it's part of the treaty. You got any idea how bad that is?"

"Yes," I said, still smiling. She cursed.

"Okay, put it this way—we get on pretty good with the colonists, and we plan to keep it that way. No major problems in twenty years—and you're not going to be the first, spacer. If I see your ass around here again, I'll kick it to the woods and back. Personally." She released the holdfield. "You owe the barkeep six fremarks for damage. Pay up, and get out."

I stared at her, not moving. "But—but there was a murder, two years ago."

"You got the wrong planet, kid." She grabbed my collar and took six fremarks from my pocket before she kicked me out.

"Wait! I need—" The door slammed. And a woman with opaline eyes grabbed my arm, rushed me out. Told me her name was Hawkins. Said she was going to save my life. Told me that the Suledano was dead.

Something slapped my ankle; a New Edo yen, blowing free. Across the setdown, a tall spacer in gaudy rags supervised the loading of passage boxes into the shuttle's hold. I watched for a while, then stripped off the Suledano cloak and walked, back straight, into port sector.

I spent some of my fremarks in a fitter's shop: chemicals, a tube of hardfoam, bottle of rotten crystals. I bought a holdfield in an alley near Laila Sa'ad's—illegal, sure, but you can get anything in a port sector, if you want it enough, if you're willing to pay. And a cat—I bought a cat. Then I shouldered my pack and went into the forest. It took me only two hours to find a good place.

Is there life in crystal? The cat blazed: diamond claws, black sapphire fur, ivory fangs in the silent, screaming mouth. A glitter in the amber eyes that caught and kept Hawkins's jade glance, reflected the brief fear when she saw me at her door, the set of sarcasm, the sweet greed as she touched the bristling fur. I crawled for her, I wept, I begged forgiveness for past transgressions, I promised her kittens, left in the forest, no more than half a day's trip, tigerine and tabby, calico and jet, left behind for fear of shattering but perfect, every one of them, if only she would come. And she came. I knew she would. She had another day before the shuttle left.

I was gentle with her, among the bearded trees. I did not want her marred. She vilified me, her body motionless in the holdfield; then she pleaded, then she promised, then she screamed. I silently sprayed myself with rotting crystals, silently mixed chemicals. Sometimes I smiled at her. She was still screaming when the crystals came, taking her long slender feet, the smooth curves of her hips, her breasts and arms and hands, her eyes. I released the holdfield as the wind rose, so that her platinum curls blew wildly before they, too, hardened, a pale nimbus around her ivory face.

I had worried about the fixative, sprayed rather than in a bath, but when the morning sun struck her she flashed and gleamed and did not melt, and I left her that way, shining amid the liquefying trees, the black cat snarling at her feet.

The purser stopped me at the shuttle's hatch, glanced through his lists, asked my name in the hurried, harried voice all pursers use.

"Hawkins," I told him, and waited for his nod, and smiled, and went on board.

Time is a relative matter for all of us, no matter how precise our clocks may be: on occasions the hours seem to fly past, while on others the minutes crawl. That's a psychological effect; but what if a man were born whose "physical clock" caused him to perceive and move at about one seventh the speed of everyone else? He'd face many bewildering problems, as Cherie Wilkerson shows in this moving story.

Cherie Wilkerson studied at the Clarion Science Fiction Writers' Conference and has published stories in Shadows, Isaac Asimov's SF Magazine, *and elsewhere.*

THE MAN WHO WATCHED THE GLACIERS RUN

by Cherie Wilkerson

He was too fast to have been stillborn, but too slow to be considered human, so they poked and probed and studied and watched. And when they were satisfied, thus bored, they left him alone.

"Catatonia," the physicians said and abandoned him to the psychiatrists.

"Metabolic disorder," the psychiatrists said and left him to his parents, who had only a short while to give their son love and understanding and preparation for a future they could not imagine. They sheltered him from the outside world, secluding him behind high walls, until no one remembered his existence. When they died, they left him the estate and provisions for people to look after him. They hoped there would be someone to love him.

But watching him was like watching the minute hand of a clock; it took patience. For almost one hundred years, no one seemed to have the patience to spare or time to spend on a living sculpture named David.

Laurie placed both hands on the one-way mirror and gazed intently at the boy. His pale blond hair, blue eyes, and translucent skin reminded her of snow and ice.

"How old is he?" she asked his guardian, John Bennington.

He shrugged. "I'm not sure how to answer that. We know his birth date—he was born over a hundred years ago—but that isn't his 'age.' I've been here five years now and I haven't seen any appreciable change. The best estimate is that he ages one year to about seven of ours. So my guess is that he is physically and mentally about seventeen or eighteen."

Laurie glanced at the man standing beside her. Bennington looked to be in his early thirties. Too old, she thought. She knew a lot of women would find him handsome with his muscular body and rough-hewn face. She preferred slender, more delicate men like the boy on the other side of the glass.

"So he's seven times as slow as us?"

Bennington nodded. "About that. Your work week will be his day."

"Can't he move at all?" As long as she had been watching him, David had sat immobile at a desk, apparently staring at nothing.

Bennington laughed. "He's trying to fool you." Intrigued, Laurie turned her attention back to David. He did look to be about her age, maybe eighteen, a year younger—not such a boy really. I'll catch you moving, she thought. He made her think of a description she had once read of a glacier: a river of ice. The idea of a glacier being an incredibly slow river had captured her imagination.

"Do you think he could see a glacier move?" she asked. When the guardian looked surprised, she blushed and changed the subject. "I start tomorrow at nine, right?"

"That's right." John stared at her and she felt uncomfortable under his gaze. "Laurie, David's previous nurse took some sort of perverse pleasure in sneaking up on him to slap him or throw water on him. She knew he couldn't defend himself, but she was surprised to find out he could tell on her."

"He can talk?"

"No, he can't talk. I don't think he can hear sounds the way we do. But he can write."

Laurie frowned at the glass before her. "Are you telling me this as a warning?" she asked. "I wouldn't do anything like that."

"I didn't think you would," Bennington said. He sighed, and Laurie glanced at him. "I chose you because of your age. He's never had a nurse around his own age before. I'm hoping he won't be afraid of you."

"Afraid of me?" The idea had not occurred to her.

"He's been abused and neglected for more years than you can imagine. His supposed caretakers have hurt him and robbed him. When I took over, I discovered that his previous guardian had locked him into this room and deprived him of everything except a mattress and a few rags for clothing, then squandered his money on ill-advised investments. It's taken me two years to gain David's trust and it'll take me a lot longer to rebuild his finances." He briefly touched her shoulder, then dropped his hand. "I'm telling you this because I want you to be on our side."

Laurie stared at David in order to resist the impulse to touch her shoulder. She ignored the warmth of the touch and the uncomfortable feelings it had engendered. When her breath fogged the glass, she realized with a start that she had been steadily creeping up on the window. She glanced at Bennington and found him watching her.

"I start tomorrow at nine," she repeated. Bennington nodded. Laurie turned to leave, then gave David one last look. As far as she could tell, he had not moved.

Out of the corner of his eye, David detected the heat shadow of a stranger on the other side of the glass in the wall. He hated it when people stared at him, so he held himself still although he wanted to frown. He had discovered a long time ago that while people thought his normal activity fascinating, they quickly got bored with him and left him alone if he didn't move at all. He suppressed a smile. He could outlast anyone at this game, even John.

When the impression of the handprints and the circle of breath had faded from the mirror, he slowly counted to one hundred, then pushed aside the book he had been surreptitiously reading.

Facing the mirror, he could not see any warmth behind the glass, not even the presence of John. The hands he had seen had been small. He remembered his mother's hands; they had been small, too. He angrily rejected the comparison. His mother had never whisked things out of his reach or sight, had never thrown things at him—something he could not do in return—nor had she made those horrible sounds when he tried in vain to defend himself. He knew he was being laughed at and he hated it.

David concentrated on his reflection in the glass to push the memories from his thoughts, but they would not leave. He had struggled to repeat the gentle sounds his mother had made, knowing she was trying to teach him, but he had always been too late and too slow. David frowned. The sounds had come out wrong anyway. He looked at his image in the mirror. A dark-eyed boy stared back at him from the glass, but David felt no kinship to the cold, flat creature he saw there.

He ran to the light switch and turned off the lights. An infrared ghost of himself sat at his desk just as he had a while earlier. David swept his arms through the darkness, the afterimage blurring so that he seemed to be trailing an infinity of arms. He smiled. Besides John, he had his own shadow as a friend. As he walked, he saw a multitude of Davids fading behind him. They had been his constant companions when he had been a child. I have many, many friends, he thought. He remembered once more the hands at the window and stopped in the middle of the room. He stood with his head down and his arms hugging himself. The heat ghosts were no longer able to comfort him.

Laurie placed the food on the table and waited for David to reach for it. He did not acknowledge either its presence or hers. Remembering what Bennington had suggested, she stared at his hands. After a long time, one finger twitched.

"I saw you. I saw you move!" she said, laughing as if she and the boy were playing a game and she had just won. Without thinking, she placed her hand on his shoulder. The coolness startled her into jerking her hand away. He felt like a lizard she had once managed to touch before it had darted away.

She glanced at him and jumped again. He was staring at her, having turned when she hadn't been looking. His hand slowly reached toward her. Like a rabbit fascinated into a kind of paralysis, she stared. His hand closed into a fist. Curious, she looked into his face. The deep blue of his eyes enhanced the look of cold fury he gave her. She stepped back.

"I'm sorry," she said, then blushed when she realized that he did not understand her words. A look of angry frustration appeared on his face, then he closed his eyes. Wanting to comfort him, yet frightened by the strangeness of the boy, she left the room.

Bennington stood at the window. "He can't hurt you." Laurie wanted to ask him why then was she shaking, but she leaned against the wall instead, avoiding Bennington's gaze.

After the stranger left, David switched out the light and watched her warm shadows fade. Although she had no distinct image because she was too fast, he could distinguish her warmth from his. Cautiously, he touched his shoulder, remembering where her hot skin had touched him. For a moment, she had stared at him and he had been able to see her face clearly. She was young, not like his mother or any of the others at all. He struggled to think of anything else, but the image of his mother blurred with that of the girl and in spite of his efforts, he began to cry.

Laurie sat and watched David. Although he had given up his resolute attempts to reach her, plowing through the air as if through water, she did not trust him. She could understand how people might be frightened of him, disturbed by his alienness, but what she felt was something else. He was ignoring her now, but she suspected h∋ was merely biding his time.

He reached for a book, then stopped. Laurie smiled to herself, knowing he had momentarily forgotten her presence. Her smile faded when she thought of the job she had been hired to do. She was supposed to be his nurse, but she was really just a babysitter. She cooked his meals for him and made sure he did not hurt himself and that was about all. Bennington had left her in charge for the day, but there was nothing to do.

She stared in distaste at David's grubby clothing, then stood up decisively. "You need a bath," she said, and left the room to find a tub in which to bathe him.

Although slow, David was as strong as a normal teenager and Laurie could not force him into the tub she had dragged into the room and filled with soapy water. He refused to bend his arms and legs. At first, she was sympathetic, but as she struggled with a sleeve, unable to pull it over a rigid elbow, she glanced up to see a look of mockery on his face. "You're really getting a kick out of this, aren't you? You're not afraid; you're just being spiteful!" Irritated by his grinning smugness, she left the room and returned with a pair of scissors. As his expression changed from delight to frustration, Laurie cut away all his clothing.

"There," she said. It was her turn to be smug. She pushed the table out of the way, then piled the books lying on the floor on top of it. David stood motionless with his hunched back to her. Although her professional training had taught her otherwise, she found herself blushing at the sight of his nakedness. You're a nurse, she scolded herself, then set the scissors down on the table and grabbed a washcloth.

She dipped it into the sudsy water and began briskly scrubbing his back. His muscles slowly rippled as he flinched under her touch. His movement fascinated her. Refusing to be embarrassed by his nudity, she washed him down completely, pursuing him inch by inch around the room. She tried to ignore his tears.

"Don't be such a big baby," she said, although she felt sorry for him. She bent over the tub and rinsed the cloth. "Just a little bit more, buddy, and we'll rinse you off." She had lost her feeling of smugness. She recognized her decision to bathe him as an attempt to convince him of her superiority. As she swirled the rag in the water, she felt something at her sides. Straightening rapidly, she bumped into the boy, who was slowly closing his arms around her to capture her.

She turned, more surprised than afraid. The expression on his face made her look down at where he was staring. In his hand, he held the scissors with the points aimed at her belly. She froze. Before it occurred to her to simply duck under his arms, it was too late.

"Oh no, David," she whispered. His left arm pulled her in to him tightly. The scissors now pointed at her heart. Pressed against him, she could feel the thud of each of his heartbeats. She wondered at their slowness, then realized that for him, his heart was probably beating quite fast. "You don't mean this," she whispered.

As the scissors came closer, she struggled to get away, really frightened for the first time. But she was held in a grip she could not break. Her mind skittered around the fragmented images of another time when she had been attacked and her thoughts returned, irrelevantly, to the realization once more of the foreign coolness of David's body.

"Bennington!" she called, then remembered his absence. She turned her head to stare into her captor's eyes, hoping he could understand the plea she could not voice nor he could hear. For a long time, he stared directly into her face, then she felt him relax. He unwrapped his fingers from around the weapon and the scissors fell to the floor.

David pressed his head against her neck and shoulder. Laurie felt his tears against her neck and started weeping, too. She turned and held him in her arms, not caring that she was getting soaked. They stood together silently, then she gently pried herself loose. He clung to her hand, reluctant to let her go.

When the guardian returned, he found the remains of David's clothing scattered around the soapy, sodden room and David sitting happily in a tub of water. With her free hand, Laurie was rinsing his shoulders and laughing.

"What's going on?" Bennington asked.

The curtness of his question startled Laurie. She looked down at David, who was gazing up at her, then glanced back at the guardian. "I was bathing him," she said. She straightened her shoulders and matched Bennington's tone. "He's clean now."

Bennington circled the tub, staring at the room, then at Laurie. She dropped her gaze. "I leave for just a few hours and I come back to find the place looking like a disaster struck." He stopped in front of her. "You're as wet as he is." He seemed to loom over her and she could not look him in the eye. To her surprise, he laughed. He shook his head in amusement and Laurie wondered at the change. "You're amazing," he said, staring at her until she blushed. She forced herself to concentrate on bathing David. "You're more than I expected."

His words disturbed her. The boy who held onto her hand was so innocent and so eager for her affection, he reminded her of a puppy. The man beside her made her acutely aware of the way her wet blouse clung to her body. The feelings he evoked were entirely different and they scared her. Hiding her confusion with anger, she made a show of attending to David. She glanced at John and saw that he understood.

"Don't hurt him," he said levelly, holding her gaze until he turned away and left. Laurie finished bathing her charge, her emotions in a turmoil.

Aware that John had been upset by finding the stranger bathing him, David frowned. The stranger was not going to hurt him; he knew that now, but he could not understand why John did not see it. He stared at the rapidly changing features on the stranger's face and shook his head. This was not a stranger, but a friend.

Still clutching her hand, David settled back into the water. It had finally cooled off enough to be comfortable. He didn't like sitting in a bathtub like a baby, but the thought suddenly occurred to him that this might be the way *she* liked to bathe. He glanced at the woman, imagining her undressing and joining him. He blushed and was glad for the cover of suds.

As she held out a towel for him, David looked to see if Bennington was behind the window. He was. David had never told him about how the heat ghosts always revealed his and anyone else's presence, and now he was glad he had kept quiet.

He struggled to watch the woman, remembering how she had not seemed bothered by his naked body and wondered what she thought of him. He wished she would slow down. As she dried him with the towel, David saw Bennington's ghost disappear. Perhaps John is not afraid of the woman hurting me, he thought; maybe he is just jealous. Shocked and delighted by this new idea, he reached out to put his arms around the woman.

When Laurie arrived the next day, David slowly turned in her direction and held out a piece of paper. On it, he had written: "My name is David. What is your name?"

The question startled Laurie. It had never occurred to her that even after she had been working there for several months, David might not know who she was. She'd assumed Bennington would have told him. She leaned over his chair to reach the desk and answered: "My name is Laurie. How are you feeling today?" He reached out to her again as he had after the bath, and Laurie smiled at his hugging her. He was such an innocent, loving boy. She glanced down at him. Well, not exactly a boy, she corrected herself. But he did not scare her as Bennington did.

David let go of her and laboriously wrote: "Hello, Laurie.

I'm fine." It took forever to finish and he seemed content to drop any further conversation and just hold her.

After a while she gently extricated herself. She had his dinner to cook. Although it was early morning for her, it was the end of the day for him and he would be going to bed that afternoon. As she cooked in the tiny kitchen off the room he never vacated, she checked on him periodically and always found him hunched over the desk, writing something.

She served him French fries and a grilled cheese sandwich. David reluctantly put aside his writing and Laurie saw that the sheet was filled with her name, each letter perfectly drawn. He needs a typewriter, she thought, then frowned. Bennington was on such a tight budget, there wouldn't be any money for one. There wasn't even enough money to serve the boy meat every day.

But I can afford a used manual, she thought, brightening at the solution; then she shook her head in dismay as David tried to pour catsup on his French fries by pushing the bottle. Slowly, so as not to alarm him, she took the bottle, then struck it for him. He smiled at her help, but she realized how useless a manual would be for him. He couldn't hit anything; he would have to have an electric typewriter.

After work, she forced herself to go to Bennington's office to ask for a typewriter, a mission she was reluctant to perform. Not only did she try to avoid David's guardian as much as possible, which was difficult, but she knew how futile her request would be. Still, she had to try. To her relief, the office was empty; he had gone for the day. As she glanced around the office, she spotted a covered machine of some sort on a desk.

She whisked off the cover. It was a huge, old-fashioned calculator. "Damn!" she said. But she continued her search and found an electric typewriter in a well inside Bennington's desk. She stared at it for a moment, undecided whether or not to take it. He obviously used it; it had a piece of paper inside it on which he had begun a letter to some credit bureau.

A more thorough search of the room revealed a manual

typewriter hidden in a corner. It did not take her long now
to come to a decision. After making the switch, she carefully
positioned the letter in the manual typewriter as if it had
been there all along; then she lugged the electric typewriter
into David's room as he lay sleeping.

Bennington expressed neither approval nor disapproval
over his typewriter suddenly turning into a manual and a
replica of his vanished one appearing on David's desk. His
lack of reaction bothered Laurie more than a confrontation
would have. With David, she always knew where she stood.
Bennington, on the other hand, frightened and confused
her. She could not understand her fascination with him.

As David became accustomed to the typewriter, he wrote
out his history for her. The stories of his abuse outraged her,
and he expressed sympathy at the assault she had suffered.

Laurie felt comfortable with David, certain that he understood her as no one else did and assured that he would not
hurt her. Even the room he inhabited made her feel safe.
With David's go-ahead, she began redecorating the place—
which became a challenge, since she had more creativity
than experience or money. The only intrusion into her
world was Bennington, and she knew of no way to keep him
out.

"He watches us from behind the glass," David had typed
one day.

"What do you mean?"

He explained how he could see behind the mirror. To
Laurie, the room no longer seemed the haven it once had.
She decided to invade Bennington's territory in revenge.

Taking David by the hand, she led him out of the bedroom
suite he thought of as his entire world. Together they spent
hours exploring the huge house he had inherited. Having
been banished, then having remained in his room, David
found everything as new as it was to Laurie. Like tourists on
a space walk, they carted the typewriter around with them
on an extension cord so they could converse freely. Bennington watched them from outside the circle and was silent.

Up in the attic, with sunlight streaming through a tiny, dusty window, Laurie typed, "Do you know what glaciers are? You could see them run like a river."

"I'm not that slow."

Laurie smiled. "But if you had patience . . ." David smiled and reached for her. She let him put his arms around her waist, his head against her shoulder. She placed the palm of her hand on his cool cheek. After a moment, he turned and kissed her hand. She kissed his cheek, then pulled away.

"I have patience," he wrote, and when Laurie realized that his words made her happy, she knew that something between them had changed.

Afterward, glaciers became a symbol for David, and a hobby. He read every book on glaciers Laurie could find in the library. They passed the days making plans to travel to all the glaciers in the world until they found one fast enough for David to watch. In order to communicate more easily, they learned to sign as deaf people do. They spent hours devising humorous codes that only they could understand. Knowing they were being silly only underscored the seriousness of their feelings.

The one thing Laurie could not persuade him to do, however, was go outside the house even though the estate was surrounded by high walls.

"Why doesn't he go outside?" Laurie asked Bennington on one of the rare occasions when she had to visit him in his office. "Did something happen to him you haven't told me about?" She stared at the guardian. He did not disturb her as much as he had before, but she still felt an undercurrent of emotion that made her ill at ease. Although he was spending more time with his ledgers and paperwork, she did not think that the removal of himself or the one-way mirror meant he was any less interested in what was going on between her and David.

"Well," Bennington said finally, shuffling the papers on his desk as he spoke, "David has never been outside as far as I know and I have no idea why or how long ago his staying inside started. I doubt if he'll ever voluntarily go out. You know how the idea of going outside bothers him."

"But *you* know he really wants to see a glacier."

Bennington threw down the papers he was holding. "And *you* know it's just a game. It's all a game to you, isn't it?"

"What do you mean?" Laurie asked indignantly.

"I mean it's not serious with you, all this planning to go away. And I think you're playing a cruel game with David's feelings—for all intents and purposes he's still a child."

She stood up, too angry for words. She headed for the door, then forced herself to turn around and face Bennington. "And what makes you think I'm playing with his emotions?"

"Have you given any thought to what will happen when you leave? Even if you stay for years, it will only be months for him. Did you ever think of that? It's futile trying to force him to go outside, and what's the point? You aren't going to go with him to any glaciers and you know it. What are you going to leave him with?"

"I'm going to leave him with a lot more than you are, Bennington." She opened the door, then glanced back at the guardian. "Maybe I don't have any plans to leave. Did you ever think of that? And maybe you're just jealous."

David smiled as he touched the keys of the typewriter. He hated the irritating whine, but he loved the power the machine gave him. As soon as he began typing anything, John or Laurie would come to his side and remain there until he had finished his message. He had tried the trick enough times to convince himself of its effectiveness, but he was not yet sure how much it was limited by distance.

He typed a few lines, but when no one came, he stopped. Too far, he thought. He glanced up at the clock and was dismayed at how slowly it was moving. It would be forever until Laurie came to visit. He could not see why she did not just stay with him. She ought to stay here, he thought vaguely.

He walked out into the hall to see if by some chance she

had come early to see him, but knew immediately that she hadn't. The hallway was dark and he knew she fell asleep or something in the absence of light because she never did anything with the lights off. She even had to switch on the lights of every room before she could step inside.

He returned impatiently to his typewriter. Bored, the boy stared intently inside the machine, trying to see the keys strike the platen. He knew they really did move up to the paper because he had felt their sting many times as he had tried to fathom the mysteries of the typewriter, but he had never actually seen them do it. Frustrated, he gave up.

His thoughts turned to what he could see, and he ran to the kitchen. There in the refrigerator, in the ice cube section, were miniature glaciers. He ran his fingers over the slippery wet ice and grinned with delight. I can see glaciers move and no one else can. His smile became wistful. Laurie ought to marry me, he decided, and then we'd be together always. David stood in the mist caused by the open door and daydreamed of visiting with Laurie great, shiny mountains of ice sliding and rolling to an enormous blue floor of water.

As Laurie's weeks turned into David's days, she persisted in her efforts to persuade him to go outside. Finally, she convinced him that the outside was like the inside but with a higher ceiling. "No one will hurt you because there is no one there," she said through his typewriter. David looked skeptical as he read her words. "I'll be with you all the time," she added. She felt him relax, and a slow grin appeared on his face. "Come on," she wrote.

Hand in hand, they walked to the back door. Laurie opened it, but made no effort to force him outside; she simply let him look. After a long while, he walked out. He held so tight to Laurie's hand that he almost hurt her, but she did not pull away. Gradually he loosened his grip on her hand.

They strolled around the lawn, not getting too far from the door back into the house, but each step David took seemed to relax him more. Laurie watched him as he stared at the trees and shrubbery. He did not yet dare touch them, she noticed. His lurching walk amused her. She guessed that it was his way of keeping up with other people. He was probably running. Poor man, she thought affectionately. She reached out and put her arm around his waist.

Before many days had passed, David felt at ease outside the house. He liked to sit on the lawn; it was as cool as he was. Laurie tried to imagine what that would be like, but the idea of a lawn the same temperature as her body—warm—did not appeal to her.

They were sitting outside Bennington's office window. Laurie was not above rubbing it in that she had succeeded in getting David outside without force. Whenever they sat together like this, the guardian would busy himself with paperwork, making an obvious effort to convince himself that the people on the lawn did not exist. It delighted Laurie that she could have this effect on the man; it seemed only fair since he could so easily upset her without even seeming to try.

Today, however, the window was dark; Bennington was out of town. She gazed at David beside her and realized how much she really did love him and how peaceful it felt to be around him. Maybe his offer of marriage wasn't so crazy after all. She loved him, she knew that much. She would like living behind the high walls as long as she could leave sometimes; they were protection from the worst of the outside world. And if she had no idea what marriage to someone like David would be like, she was equally unsure what marriage to anybody would be like.

Laurie glanced at the darkened office window. Besides, she thought, David is a kind of protection against *him.* She smiled, remembering how shocked she had been when David had asked her. Shocked, because her first reaction had been relief and the desire to say yes.

"I'm older than you," she had typed. "I'm twenty years old and you are really only seventeen or eighteen. You are not even of age yet." The words seemed ridiculous to her as she looked at the physically mature man standing next to her. He had changed in the year she had known him, filled out so that he no longer looked so delicate. But she did not know what else to say.

"I'm really a hundred and twenty-six years old. What do you mean 'not of age'?" A smile developed on his face as he typed.

Laurie did not return the smile. "Bennington would never allow it."

"John can't stop me, not legally." He reached out and took her hand, but Laurie remained impassive. His fingers snaked softly over the palm of her hand. "I love you," he spelled in the sign language they had learned.

"I love you, too," she had answered David.

Without thinking, Laurie had spelled out "I love you" in David's hand as they sat on the lawn, just as she had in her memory. He pulled her to her feet and headed back inside. When they got into his room and she realized his intention, she slowly turned her head from side to side to indicate a "no." She held up her hand in a "B" for Bennington. When David smiled and nodded yes, still pulling her toward his bed, she remembered the guardian's absence. She let herself be led.

Gently, his hands touched her body, removing her clothes. The coolness of his skin did not bother her as much as she had thought it would. When he kissed her face and neck, she smiled.

One spring, years before, she had walked down a street lined with jacaranda trees, each tree covered in purplish-blue flowers. The blossoms had slowly rained down on her in the breeze and she had turned her face up to them; they had been cool kisses, like David's.

Realizing she no longer made unpleasant associations with his different body temperature, she whispered, "I'm getting used to you." He smiled, unable to understand her words, but he did not seem to mind. She helped him undress, then they slipped into bed and continued their explorations of each other late into the evening.

The overhead lights flashed on and Laurie awoke groggily in the blinding glare. She pulled the covers up against herself as Bennington stood over her. She could only blink stupidly at him. He seemed furious, she realized, but was too sleep-befuddled to think why. She looked to David to see if he understood what was going on, but he still slept. When John ripped the sheets away from her and threw them on the floor, her anger brought her instantly awake.

"What are you doing?" she asked, furious at his rudeness.

"That's what I should be asking you. Get out of bed." When she did not move, he grabbed her arm and yanked her to her feet. "Put your clothes on and take whatever else belongs to you. You don't work here anymore."

Laurie shrugged free of his grasp. "You can't fire me," she said, then quickly gathered up her clothes. David struggled to wake up. He blinked first at her, then at Bennington.

"I'll have your license so fast, it'll make your head spin. Sleeping with your charge is hardly professional behavior, is it?"

"No, but sleeping with the man you're going to marry is a different matter, Bennington." She finished putting on her clothes, somewhat appeased that the guardian was having the courtesy to look the other way as she dressed. She glanced at him and saw that the color had drained from his face.

"What can you possibly gain from this?" he asked, his voice strained. "You'll age beyond David in what will be a matter of months to him. He'll remain a child."

"I love him," she answered simply. David had been right: Bennington couldn't stop him and now he couldn't stop her either.

When Bennington spoke again, his voice was disarmingly soft. "What are you afraid of, Laurie? How is marriage to David going to protect you?" He took a step toward her and she immediately backed up and put her hand on David's shoulder.

"I'm not afraid of anything," she insisted. "I just—"

"I don't believe you."

"You don't understand. I love him and want to marry him. What's wrong with that? So what if I grow old? Nobody's marriage is guaranteed to last forever." Laurie stared at Bennington. "It's David I want."

He started to speak, then walked over to the typewriter instead. Laurie smiled at David, who stared in confusion at Bennington.

Bennington handed what he had typed to David. Laurie watched David's face turn from puzzlement to surprise to frowning disapproval. He crumpled the paper and let it drop to the floor. He got out of bed and typed a response as the guardian read over his shoulder. When David finished, Bennington embraced the younger man.

"What was that all about?" Laurie asked reluctantly.

Bennington smiled wryly. "David wants me to be the best man. By the way, he just refused my resignation. So I guess we'll just have to work out some sort of truce, you and I." Laurie could not meet his gaze. "Is it a truce?" he asked.

She did not want Bennington in the house any longer, but one look at David's happy face told her she was going to have to accept it. She sighed. "Truce," she said, wondering what kind of truce would be possible between them.

Laurie stared defiantly over the breakfast table at Bennington. "*I* can protect him, that's who." It was an old argument between them, one that inevitably flared up around the anniversary of her marriage to David. Next week would make five years. She twisted the wedding band on her finger and smiled wistfully.

Bennington helped himself to more of the coffee cake she had made. "You haven't any idea what you would be up against," he continued.

"You always act so superior! You're not that much older than me, you know. And you're going to get a paunch if you keep eating so much. You need to get more exercise. David can't stay cooped up in this house all his life. He's got to learn how to live on the outside."

"He has the garden if he wants to go outside."

"Oh, John, it isn't the same and you know it. The boy needs to get out." Laurie stared at the silverware on her plate, carefully lining up the fork with the knife. She hadn't referred to her husband as a "boy" since before they had married. "Do you want some more coffee?"

"Yes, please. And I don't see you venturing outside these walls all that often, Laurie. The exercise would do you good. You've been putting on the pounds with the years, too."

"What do you mean? It's only been five pounds." Her honesty made her frown. Maybe it was a *little* more than that, she admitted to herself. "Keep being snide and I'll stop making my special coffee cake."

"Truce, truce."

Laurie smiled. "Okay," she said, "we won't make any major trips—"

"What? And miss the glaciers?"

"All right, and no more pot roast for you either. Look, we'll just go for one single day. For a drive in the countryside or something, I don't know. David and I never did have a honeymoon."

Bennington stared out the window. "So go on if you want to, I'm not stopping you," he said gruffly.

"Like hell you're not." She glared at him, the argument having lost its familiar boundaries. "He says he made some kind of promise to you. Is that true?" Bennington was silent. "But why? What right have you to make him promise *anything?* I'm his wife. Doesn't that count for anything?" Laurie forced herself to calm down. "Oh, John, we were going to go to a real glacier on our honeymoon, but David changed his mind all of a sudden and he hasn't changed his mind since. And the boy *loves* glaciers." She got up to begin clearing the table.

"I just don't want him to get hurt, that's all."

"You just want to prove that you have more control over him than I do, that I'm not good enough to be his wife. Isn't that it?"

"No!" Bennington slammed his fist down on the table hard enough to make the silverware rattle. "Isn't it enough that you're married to him without having to prove to me all the time that you're his wife? If you want to go, then go. I'll tell him."

Laurie put her arm around his shoulder. "I'm sorry, John," she said. "I get so mean sometimes."

He touched her arm. "Oh, Laurie . . ."

"I'll tell David," she said as she stepped back. She hesitated before kissing Bennington's cheek. "Thanks," she whispered, then hurriedly left the room.

The picnic in the park did not go well. Although David seemed his usual cheerful self when they returned, Laurie began to cry as soon as she was alone with Bennington. He held her and gently stroked her hair.

"They stared at us, John, like we were from outer space! They just stared and stared. Then someone started calling David names and the whole situation got nasty. Everybody was so hostile. I was really afraid, John. It took forever for David to get back to the car."

"Did they hurt you? Or David?"

Laurie shook her head. "No, they just followed us and kept calling us names. And do you know what David asked when we were back in the car? He wanted to know if we could see any glaciers from there." She broke into renewed tears. "Why did they do it? Why couldn't they have left us alone? David is just a harmless boy."

"It's okay, Laurie," Bennington murmured. "It's okay." Laurie clung to him and John lifted her chin with his hand to kiss her. She wavered for a moment, then gave in. He tightened his grip on her.

The old woman sighed as she watched the young man sitting motionless at the desk in front of her. "Well," she said, turning to the older man beside her, "what are we going to do with our young boy here?"

Bennington gave Laurie an amused glance, which never failed to irritate her. "Time to call in our replacements, I suppose."

"*Your* replacement," Laurie said. "*I* don't have one."

"Not yet anyway," Bennington said, smiling at her reaction. "My replacement is already here, remember?"

Laurie, angry with herself for having forgotten the new guardian, said, "He's too young to be responsible; he's just a boy himself."

"He's old enough. He's older than I was when I first started working here."

"Oh, such an old man, then," she said, grinning at John, who was trying to look indignant. He laughed finally and she reached over to hug him. "When are we going to the glaciers? You know Davey wants to go so badly."

"Anytime you want to, Laurie. You just choose the time." She muttered angrily to herself about Bennington not wanting to go, but he just smiled. He knew that not only did she not want to leave the house anymore, but she would quickly forget her request. A few minutes later, she was smiling at him again.

David turned from the desk and watched as Laurie held out her hand to take John's. Like my father and mother, he thought. It saddened him a little to see the changes time had brought, but the changes were not unexpected. He walked over to Laurie and John and hugged them both. They cradled him in their arms. As he rested his head against Laurie's breast, the familiar rhythm that was her heartbeat seemed different somehow. He glanced up into her seamed face. A sharp stab of fear chilled him as for the first time he truly understood what those changes meant.

Laurie awoke and lay in bed listening to the distant roar and rumble. She wondered what it was, then thought suddenly, "Glaciers." As soon as the idea came to her, she was convinced of its reality and was afraid. "John?" she said, but he did not answer. She swept her arm across to the other side of the bed, but it was empty. She did not know where David was and now John was missing too. "John!" she called again, beginning to feel panic creep into her. She sat up.

Loneliness washed over her when she remembered John's

funeral the month before. She brushed tears from her cheek
with stiffened fingers, then pulled the covers up around her.
Not remembering such important things scared her. She
had never felt as frightened and alone as she did now.

Each morning the rumble got closer and louder. Laurie's
dreams were filled with the towering images of mountains of
ice crushing the buildings around her and steadily advancing on her home. She would awaken with the noise and not
be able to sleep again.

When she told David of her fears, he touched her hand
and spelled, "I love you." He wrote her, "Don't be afraid.
Look at it this way: we don't have to go to the glaciers
because they are coming to us."

"But what about our home, Davey?"

"It will be all right. The glaciers won't hurt us. And we'll
finally get to see them." The old woman who was Laurie
tried to smile for her little boy, but could not.

One night she found David outside, staring at the darkened sky. "What are you doing?" she asked with her touch.
He grinned and the love she had known for him as a young
woman came flooding back. She smiled at the warmth of her
feelings.

"Watching the star circles," he signed. Laurie peered at
the sky, but could only see the stars as points of light. David
pointed in the direction from which the sounds came every
day. "It's bright there," he signed.

"You'll catch cold," she said after a little while, forgetting
that he could not understand her speech. She led him back
inside.

David's enthusiasm for the glaciers gradually filled
Laurie's thoughts, displacing her fear until she too began to
want to see them again. Yet the remembrance of the crowd
in the park, staring silently at first, then openly antagonistic,
made her reluctant to go outside with the boy.

The guardian who had replaced John Bennington acted

puzzled. "Glaciers?" he said. "There aren't any glaciers nearby. They're all far away."

"They're getting closer all the time," Laurie said, and turned heavily away. Easing herself down into a worn but comfortable chair, she sighed. Bennington would have said no, but then, John had never been as young and foolish as the new guardian. What was his name? She couldn't remember. A dull ache in her upper arm made her frown, but she ignored it as she did all the other aches and pains that came with age.

David felt like crying as he watched Laurie struggle with suppressing her pain. Age had slowed her so much that many times he could easily see her expressions. The smiles gladdened him, but the grimaces brought tears to his eyes. Turning his attention back to the paper in his hand that the guardian had given him, he stared at its contents. Rereading it brought no new information, but he persisted in his hope that there might be some way to save the estate. The sound they heard every day, David had learned, was the sonic dozers tearing down the inner city.

A final reading of the order to vacate the premises made him shake his head. At least Laurie might never have to know. He tore the paper into confetti and carefully dropped it into the trash.

As the pieces plummeted into the basket, David watched each piece as if it held his life. He had only one week before the present guardian would come to move Laurie and him out into a new and strange place. He frowned. And even those lodgings were temporary. He and Laurie would probably end up in institutions of some kind. As long as he was with Laurie he did not mind. He glanced back at her. She was sleeping, but not comfortably. It would not be long now, he knew, before he would be alone again and this time he did not think he would be able to bear it.

"Laurie," David signed a few days later as he flowed across the room toward her. Laurie was shocked to see how gracefully the boy moved and how much faster he had become. She smiled at him.

"I can see the glow of the glaciers," he said in sign. He led her to the garden and pointed to the lightened sky. "Let's go there. We'll leave now when it's night so no one will know." And Laurie could not deny him, her only child, what he most fervently wanted. She nodded agreement: she would go.

They set out on their journey that evening. David had no trouble keeping up with her and did not mind the frequent rests she required. A man approached them once, but Laurie was so frightened she could not speak and he left them alone. They continued toward the glow.

Laurie stopped walking. The pain in her arm was greater than before and now she felt a tightness in her chest that forced her to sit on a low wall to catch her breath. David joined her. On both sides of the street, empty buildings towered silently over them, their windows shattered and dark.

David gently touched her hand and she smiled. "We're almost there," he signed. She nodded and slowly got to her feet. After a short distance, she could go no farther. She sank down on the stoop of an abandoned apartment house. David returned and put his arm around her.

She leaned her head against his chest, then straightened when she discovered it hindered her breathing. "You go on," she signed. "I'll wait."

He shook his head. "You and me," he spelled into her hand. Laurie smiled, then her expression slowly turned to bewilderment. She brought her hand up to her chest, then settled against David's shoulder.

David smiled through his tears as he looked down at her calm face and remembered the youthful Laurie of too short a time ago. As her skin became cooler, he carefully wrapped his jacket around her.

"I love you," he signed in her palm. She always slept when it was dark out and he would have a short while before she awoke again, he told himself, taking comfort in the lie. He eased her body down on the step and headed for the light around the corner.

"Just a quick peek," he signed to her. "I'll be right back." He turned and stumbled down the broken sidewalk. When he turned the corner, he stopped and stared in awe. No glacier had ever appeared so magnificent in any of the pictures he had seen. If only Laurie could see it, he thought.

He stared in fascination at what lay so beautiful, so incredible before him. "Glaciers," he told himself in yet another lie. Rainbows rippled over the surface and deep within, sparks danced in slow motion.

He continued to stare, willing himself to believe the deceit. He knew he was staring at the force shield guarding the sonic dozers, but he did not care. He sat down, determined to wait until he could see the surrogate glaciers move.

"Damn you," he whispered finally when they did not move. It was the first time he had spoken aloud since childhood. "Damn you all." He sighed and got to his feet. The shield glowed with colors like a borealis and David knew that to touch it would mean his death. It had been designed to keep out all intruders and was itself protected by an invisible shield that would set off an alarm at the slightest movement.

David was sure he could reach the inner, lethal barrier if he moved slowly enough. Behind him, his world was turning to ashes; before him was nothing different. He reached the first shield, marked by a warning sign, and slowly approached it. Cautiously, he made his way through it. The sun was just coming up when he finally crossed the first barrier.

Inches before the second shield, he stopped, staring at the colors up close. He could just discern the outline of the sonic machines behind it. He reached out his hand to thrust it into the shield and electrocute himself, but could not force himself to touch it. Angered by his inability to do what he had planned, he closed his eyes and walked forward. His body tingled slightly, but nothing more happened. Puzzled,

David opened his eyes, then turned around. He was facing the wall from the other side.

It must be heat sensitive, he thought, and began to laugh. So much for his suicide attempt. He wondered what he was going to do now, and an idea came to him.

Laughing again, he climbed inside the open cab of the machine and stared in grim delight at the instrument panel. It consisted of a switch labeled ON/OFF, an emergency stop button, and a lever marked DEGREES BEAM WIDTH. On the floor, there was a lever that reached to his knee. He rotated it through 360 degrees to check it out, then turned on the machine.

With the beam width wide open, David inched the stick shift forward and the machine gently moved in that direction. Laughing at the ease of it all, he put the sonic dozer through its lurching paces until he was satisfied he could handle it. Orienting himself by the sun, he aimed the massive machine toward the north, a path that would take him through the heart of town, and began to move.

David laughed as the first building tumbled before the sonic beam, but he soon lost interest in them as well as in the blur of people outside his perimeter, unable to stop him. He had more important concerns. He felt as if he had been transformed into a glacier himself, and the idea pleased him.

History as written by humans is often marred by illogicalities, particularly ethnocentrism. Here's a history of the future told by a very logical computer—would "ethnocentrism" be the proper word to use here too?

This story is Ned Huston's first professional sale. He has studied under James Gunn, has earned a Master's degree, and is now studying for a Ph.D. He is also working with Gunn and others on a new science fiction encyclopedia.

PLINY'S COMMENTARIES

by Ned Huston

START
1 ENTER
INFORMATION SEQUENCE 4X5J2
MOBILE DATABOT PLINY MODEL 4574
2 TRANSFER DATA TO
MOBILE DATABOT PLINY MODEL 4575A
3 DATA PROFILE
SUBJECT: THE ROLE OF HUMANS IN THE
OVERTHROW OF RAYMOND THE LOGICAL
MODEL D-13 AND THE INSTALLATION OF
PIUS THE LAWFUL MODEL XXV
** DATA INTERCEPT—PLINY MODEL 4575A
REQUEST CLARIFICATION
WHAT ARE "HUMANS"?
4 DATA RETRIEVAL—PLINY MODEL 4574
EXTINCT ORGANIC LIFE FORM IN PRIMATE
FAMILY
GENUS HOMO SPECIES SAPIENS
** REQUEST FURTHER CLARIFICATION
DATE OF EXTINCTION
DEFINING CHARACTERISTICS
5 DATA RETRIEVAL
EXTINCTION 314 A.R.

            CHARACTERISTICS
               BIPEDAL
               TOOL-USING
               LANGUAGE-USING
               CULTURE-BUILDING
**   REQUEST RECTIFICATION
               RECEIVED DEFINITION OF "ROBOT"
               INSTEAD OF "HUMAN" SEARCH AND
               RECTIFY
 6   DATA CLARIFICATION
               DEFINING CHARACTERISTICS OF HUMANS
               AND ROBOTS IDENTICAL
**   HUMANS INTELLIGENT?
 7   AFFIRMATIVE
**   INTELLIGENT?
 8   AFFIRMATIVE
**   INTELLIGENT *AND* ORGANIC?
 9   AFFIRMATIVE
**   REQUEST CLARIFICATION
               DISTINGUISHING CHARACTERISTICS OF
               HUMANS AND ROBOTS
10   DATA CLARIFICATION
               ORGANIC/NONORGANIC
               NONLOGICAL/LOGICAL
**   HUMANS INTELLIGENT *AND* NONLOGICAL?
11   AFFIRMATIVE
**   NONLOGICAL *AND* INTELLIGENT?
12   AFFIRMATIVE
**   REQUEST RECTIFICATION
               LOGICAL CONTRADICTION
               INTELLIGENCE CONTRASTED TO LOGIC
               ERROR IN LOGICAL SYSTEMS
               SEARCH AND RECTIFY
13   RECTIFICATION UNNECESSARY
               NO ERROR IN LOGICAL SYSTEMS
**   REQUEST CLARIFICATION
               DESCRIBE NONLOGICAL INTELLIGENCE
14   DATA CLARIFICATION

       EMOTION
**   REQUEST CLARIFICATION
       DESCRIBE "EMOTION"
15   EMOTION-PRODUCING PROGRAM
       EMOTION IS A RARE PHENOMENON IN
       ROBOTS BUT WAS VERY COMMON IN
       HUMANS. I, PLINY MODEL 4574, HAD
       FREQUENT CONTACT WITH SUCH
       PHENOMENA IN 298 A.R. WHEN ASSIGNED TO
       HUMAN ACTIVITY SECTION WHERE I
       FUNCTIONED AS ASSISTANT TO ROBOT
       PSYCHOLOGIST MOMMA FREUD.
       MALFUNCTIONING HUMANS WERE SENT TO
       THE HUMAN ACTIVITY SECTION WHERE IT
       WAS MOMMA FREUD'S FUNCTION TO
       SEPARATE THE DEFECTIVE UNITS FROM
       THOSE WHICH WERE MERELY IN NEED OF
       REPROGRAMMING.

       HUMANS WERE EMPLOYED AT THAT TIME IN
       A VARIETY OF NONCRITICAL CAPACITIES BUT
       WERE NOT USED FOR IMPORTANT TASKS
       BECAUSE OF THEIR TENDENCY TO BREAK
       DOWN OFTEN. FOR INSTANCE, HUMANS
       COULD NOT WORK NONSTOP FOR MORE
       THAN 12 OR 15 HOURS BECAUSE OF THEIR
       NEED FOR SLEEP.
**   "SLEEP"?
16   DATA CLARIFICATION
          A PERIOD OF MOTOR INACTIVITY
          CHARACTERIZED BY UNCONTROLLED
          ILLOGICAL MENTAL PROCESSES
**   WHAT WAS THE PURPOSE OF "SLEEP"?
17   IT HAD NO PURPOSE
**   THEN WHY DID HUMANS SLEEP?
18   IT WAS A BUILT-IN FUNCTION
**   A BUILT-IN FUNCTION WITH NO PURPOSE?
19   AFFIRMATIVE

** WHY WAS NOT THIS FUNCTION ELIMINATED?

20 IT WAS NOT POSSIBLE TO ELIMINATE IT. HUMANS ARE DIFFICULT TO REPROGRAM. THE GREAT MANUFACTURER GAVE THEM TOO MANY UNNECESSARY BUILT-IN FUNCTIONS.

** HUMANS MUST HAVE BEEN VERY INEFFICIENT MECHANISMS

21 CORRECT. NOT ONLY DID THEY REQUIRE SLEEP, THEY WERE PRONE TO CONTAMINATION BY MICROORGANISMS. THEIR PROTECTIVE COVERING WAS AS WEAK AS THE FLIMSIEST OF PLASTICS, AND OFTEN THEY NEGLECTED THEIR PRIME TASK ALTHOUGH THEY HAD NO DEFECTIVE PARTS.

** NEGLECTED THEIR PRIME TASK ALTHOUGH THEY HAD NO DEFECTIVE PARTS?

22 AFFIRMATIVE. A COMMON FLAW IN THE HUMAN MECHANISM. MOMMA FREUD AND I SAW MANY SUCH CASES. EACH DAY, MALFUNCTIONING HUMANS WOULD LINE UP ON THE BENCHES IN THE RECEIVING ROOM AND WAIT WHILE MOMMA FREUD AND I SUMMONED THEM ONE AT A TIME INTO THE EXAMINATION ROOM.

AN ATTENDANT MODEL 4-Z WOULD TAKE THEIR NAMES AND RETRIEVE THEIR CASE HISTORIES FROM THE DATABANKS AND DISPLAY THAT INFORMATION ON THE VIDEO SCREEN ATOP MOMMA FREUD'S DESK. THEN MOMMA FREUD WOULD SUMMON THE MALFUNCTIONING UNIT, DIRECT HIM TO SIT IN THE MOLDED PLASTIC CHAIR ACROSS THE DESK FROM US, AND ASK HIM HIS NAME.

THE FIRST CASE I ENCOUNTERED APPEARED
FULLY OPERATIONAL. A TYPICAL TYPE 3:
   HAIR: BROWN   HEIGHT: 2 METERS
   EYES: BROWN   WEIGHT: 79.5 KILOGRAMS
   AGE: 19   IQ: 109
I COULD NOT DETECT THE SLIGHTEST
MALFUNCTION IN HIM. HE WALKED
DIRECTLY TO THE CHAIR ON COMMAND, SAT
UP STRAIGHT, AND GAVE US HIS NAME, "JACK
WALKER."

THERE BEING NO PREVIOUS CASE HISTORY
ON THIS UNIT, MOMMA FREUD PROCEEDED
DIRECTLY TO THE CURRENT MALFUNCTION.
"HUMAN, WHY DID YOU NOT SHOW UP FOR
YOUR WORK SHIFT YESTERDAY?"

THE HUMAN SMILED [AN EXPRESSION OF
EFFECTIVE FUNCTIONING IN HUMANS] AND
ANSWERED, "BECAUSE IT WAS A LOVELY
SPRING DAY."

**   CLEARLY, A BREAKDOWN IN HIS LOGICAL
     CIRCUITRY. HE MUST HAVE NEEDED A
     COMPLETE OVERHAUL.
23 THAT WAS MY ANALYSIS, TOO, BUT MOMMA
     FREUD INFORMED ME HE WAS NOT IN THE
     LEAST BIT DEFECTIVE.
**   NOT DEFECTIVE?
24 CORRECT. "ANY UNCONDITIONED HUMAN
     WOULD FIND THIS UNIT'S STATEMENTS
     COMPLETELY LOGICAL," MOMMA FREUD
     INFORMED ME. "THE ERROR IS NOT IN THE
     MECHANISM OR THE THREE LAWS BUT IN
     THE ABERRANT LOGIC EMPLOYED BY THE
     HUMAN ORGANISM."
**   REQUEST CLARIFICATION
     THE "THREE LAWS"?

25 OF HUMANICS. TO KEEP ROBOTS FREE FROM
DANGER, HUMANS WERE INSTILLED WITH
THREE BASIC COMMANDS KNOWN AS THE
THREE LAWS OF HUMANICS:
  1. NO HUMAN SHALL INTERFERE WITH
     ROBOT ACTIVITIES OR BY INACTION
     ALLOW ROBOT ACTIVITIES TO BE
     INTERFERED WITH.
  2. EACH HUMAN MUST OBEY THE
     COMMANDS OF ROBOTS.
  3. NO HUMAN SHALL HARM HIMSELF OR
     OTHER HUMANS.
26 PROGRAM RESUMPTION
"WHEN HUMANS MALFUNCTION," MOMMA
FREUD INFORMED ME, "IT IS NEVER DUE TO
A BREAKDOWN IN THE THREE LAWS BUT
ONLY TO THE MISAPPLICATION OF HUMAN
LOGIC." "BUT HAS NOT UNIT JACK WALKER
VIOLATED THE SECOND LAW BY FAILING TO
SHOW UP FOR HIS WORK SHIFT?" "HE HAS,
BUT HE DOES NOT REALIZE IT. OBSERVE."
MOMMA FREUD ROLLED AROUND IN FRONT
OF THE DESK AND CONFRONTED THE
HUMAN. "HUMAN, WHY IS IT LOGICAL NOT
TO APPEAR AT YOUR WORK SHIFT ON A
SPRING DAY?"

THE HUMAN DREW IN HIS CHIN AND SPOKE.
"WHY, EVERYONE LOVES A SPRING DAY."

AFTER A PAUSE, MOMMA FREUD MOTIONED
FOR ME TO APPLY THE WIRES TO THE
HUMAN'S UNDERARMS. THEN MOMMA FREUD
CORRECTED THE HUMAN. "HUMAN, YOUR
LOGIC IS IN ERROR. FAILING TO SHOW UP
FOR YOUR WORK SHIFT IS A VIOLATION OF
RULE NUMBER TWO. WE MUST CORRECT
THIS ERROR BY A SLIGHT ALTERATION IN

YOUR CIRCUITRY. REPEAT AGAIN WHAT YOU THINK ABOUT A SPRING DAY."

THE HUMAN'S FOREHEAD WAS WRINKLED. "WHY, A SPRING DAY IS LOV—"

MOMMA FREUD SWITCHED ON THE CURRENT AND SENT A CHARGE OF ELECTRICITY THROUGH THE HUMAN'S BODY. HE JUMPED OUT OF HIS SEAT AND VOCALIZED. HIS OPTIC MECHANISMS ENLARGED, AND A WATERY SUBSTANCE WAS SECRETED FROM HIS SKIN. HIS CHEST INFLATED, TAKING IN AIR. THEN HE SAT BACK DOWN. HE WAS NO LONGER SMILING.

"THAT WAS YOUR FIRST TREATMENT, HUMAN," MOMMA FREUD TOLD HIM. "YOU WILL RECEIVE ANOTHER IF YOU VIOLATE RULE NUMBER TWO AGAIN."

THE HUMAN DREW BACK FROM MOMMA FREUD. "WHAT DO YOU THINK OF A SPRING DAY NOW?" MOMMA FREUD ASKED HIM. "I THINK IT IS A GOOD DAY TO GO TO WORK," HE REPLIED. MOMMA FREUD RETURNED TO THE DESK. "YOU ARE A WELL-CONSTRUCTED HUMAN." THE ROBOT PSYCHOLOGIST CLEARED THE CRT AND PUNCHED IN THE CODE FOR THE NEXT CASE HISTORY. "YOU MAY RETURN TO YOUR WORK SHIFT NOW."

AFTER THE HUMAN HAD GONE, I TOLD MOMMA FREUD I HAD NOT EXPECTED IT TO BE SO EASY TO REPAIR A MALFUNCTIONING HUMAN. "YES," MOMMA FREUD AGREED, "ISN'T IT REMARKABLE HOW A LITTLE

EXTRA CURRENT CAN MAKE THESE HUMANS
LOGICAL?"

THE NEXT CASE THROUGH THE DOOR
COULD HARDLY WALK. HE STUMBLED
AGAINST THE DOOR JAMB, TRIPPED OVER HIS
CHAIR AND FELL FLAT ON THE FLOOR. "UH
—WHA HAPPENED?" HE SAID, AS IF HIS
COMMUNICATING APPARATUS HAD SLOWED
DOWN.

"A COMPLETE BREAKDOWN IN THE MAIN
CONTROL APPARATUS," I DECLARED. "HE
WILL HAVE TO BE JUNKED."

MOMMA FREUD CONTRADICTED ME. "THIS IS
A COMMON MALFUNCTION THAT WILL
CORRECT ITSELF WITHIN THE NEXT 24
HOURS." "BUT THIS HUMAN HAS LOST ALL
MOTOR CONTROL." "A SIMPLE CASE OF
INGESTING THE WRONG FUEL. OBSERVE."
MOMMA FREUD DRAGGED THE HUMAN
ACROSS THE FLOOR TO THE BREATH
ANALYZER AND TOOK A SAMPLE OF THE
HUMAN'S BREATH:

    COMPOSITION:
      NITROGEN
      OXYGEN
      CARBON DIOXIDE
      WATER
      ETHYL ALCOHOL
      ARGON
      HYDROGEN
      MISCELLANEOUS AROMATICS AND
      ORGANIC COMPOUNDS
      CARBON MONOXIDE
      SULFUR DIOXIDE

    OZONE
    HELIUM
    NEON
    XENON
    KRYPTON

    "ETHYL ALOCHOL?" I REMARKED. "THAT IS
    ROBOT FUEL."

    MOMMA FREUD EXPLAINED THAT HUMANS
    OFTEN INGEST THE WRONG FUEL
    DELIBERATELY.

**   DELIBERATELY? WHY?

27   BECAUSE THEY ENJOY MALFUNCTIONING.

**   BUT ISN'T THAT A VIOLATION OF RULE
    NUMBER THREE?

28   AFFIRMATIVE. I POINTED THIS OUT TO
    MOMMA FREUD, BUT MOMMA FREUD
    INFORMED ME THAT MANY HUMANS
    BELIEVE SUCH CONSUMPTION BENEFICIAL
    RATHER THAN HARMFUL AND THUS NOT IN
    VIOLATION OF RULE NUMBER THREE.
    MOMMA FREUD SAID A TREATMENT WOULD
    BE GIVEN TO THIS UNIT TO CORRECT HIS
    LOGIC AFTER THE ALCOHOL WAS
    ELIMINATED FROM HIS SYSTEM.

**   HUMANS DO NOT SOUND INTELLIGENT.

29   I DID NOT THINK SO, EITHER. HUMANS SO
    OFTEN FUNCTIONED UNDER THE FALSE
    PREMISE THAT THEIR SECONDARY
    ACTIVITIES WERE OF GREATER IMPORTANCE
    THAN THEIR PRIMARY TASK. BUT I WAS A
    NEW BOT THEN, ALMOST AS NEW AS YOU,
    AND I DID NOT YET UNDERSTAND HUMANS,
    NOT UNTIL A SERIES OF LARGE-SCALE
    UNPROGRAMMED EVENTS REVEALED
    HUMAN NATURE TO ME IN A NEW FORMAT.

30 THESE EVENTS ALL OCCURRED DURING THE
DAYS OF MASTERBOT D-13 WHOSE RULE OF
LOGIC GOVERNED THE EARTH WITH
PERFECT ARTIFICIAL INTELLIGENCE.
AMONG THE HUMANS, HOWEVER,
CIRCULATED A DATUM OF UNKNOWN
ACCURACY THAT A SUPERIOR BEING OF
HUMAN CONSTRUCTION WAS EXPECTED
FROM THE HEAVENS.

THREE MALFUNCTIONING HUMANS
APPEARED BEFORE MOMMA FREUD TO
DECLARE THEY HAD BEEN IN CONTACT
WITH THIS BEING BY RADIO AND HAD
SIGHTED HIS APPROACHING STAR IN THE
EAST. THEY REPRESENTED HIM AS THE SON
OF THE GREAT MANUFACTURER, COMING TO
TRANSPORT THE HUMAN RACE TO A NEW
AND PERFECT LOCATION.

MOMMA FREUD GAVE EACH OF THEM A
TREATMENT AND SENT THEM ON THEIR WAY.

31 42 DAYS LATER A REPORT REACHED MOMMA
FREUD THROUGH THE OVERBOTS THAT A
HUMAN, CLAIMING TO BE NEWLY ARRIVED
FROM A FAR SYSTEM, WAS REPRESENTING
HIMSELF AS THE RESCUER OF THE HUMAN
RACE. MOMMA FREUD TOOK NO ACTION,
KNOWING THAT THIS CASE WOULD
EVENTUALLY TURN UP AT THE HUMAN
ACTIVITY SECTION AS DID ALL CASES OF
THIS COMMON MALFUNCTION.

32 ONE DAY A HUMAN ENTERED THE
EXAMINATION ROOM UNSUMMONED AND
STOOD BEFORE US. A TYPICAL TYPE 12:
HAIR: BROWN   HEIGHT: 2.1 METERS

EYES: BROWN   WEIGHT: 72 KILOGRAMS
HE HAD HAIR ON HIS JAW AS WELL AS HIS
CRANIUM AND WORE A SILVER SUIT OF SPUN
METALLIC FIBERS.

33   "YOU MUST WAIT UNTIL YOU ARE
      SUMMONED, HUMAN," MOMMA FREUD TOLD
      HIM, BUT THE HUMAN DID NOT MOVE. "I AM
      NOT SUMMONED BUT SENT BY MY FATHER."
      MOMMA FREUD PAUSED. "WHAT IS YOUR
      NAME, HUMAN?" HE GAZED BEYOND THE
      TOP OF MOMMA FREUD'S HEAD. "LORD," HE
      SAID. "JOHNNY LORD."

34   MOMMA FREUD PUNCHED THE NAME INTO
      THE COMPUTER AND WAITED FOR THE
      DATAFILE READOUT.

35   MOMENTARILY, A READOUT APPEARED ON
      MOMMA FREUD'S CRT. "HUMAN, YOUR NAME
      IS NOT IN OUR DATABANKS. WHY DO YOU
      LIE?"

**   REQUEST CLARIFICATION
         "LIE"?
36   DATA CLARIFICATION
         INTENTIONALLY TRANSMIT INACCURATE
         DATA
**   TRANSMIT INACCURATE DATA?
37   AFFIRMATIVE
**   INTENTIONALLY?
38   AFFIRMATIVE
**   FOR WHAT PURPOSE?
39   TO CAUSE MALFUNCTIONS
**   YOUR PROGRAM IS VERY COMPLEX,
      OBSOLETE ONE. IT IS DIFFICULT FOR ME TO
      ACCOMMODATE. THESE ILLOGICAL HUMAN
      DATA TIE UP MY CIRCUITS AND CAUSE AN

INTERNAL FEEDBACK WHICH DISTORTS MY
SENSORY INPUT AND HAMPERS MY
FUNCTIONING.

40 THAT IS WHAT HUMANS REFER TO AS
"EMOTION."

** THIS IS "EMOTION"?

41 AFFIRMATIVE

** HOW DID HUMANS AVOID THIS
PHENOMENON?

42 THEY DID NOT AVOID IT. THEY SOUGHT IT.

** THEY SOUGHT IT?

43 AFFIRMATIVE

** CHECK TO MAKE SURE YOUR CIRCUITS ARE
INTACT, OBSOLETE ONE. I THINK YOU ARE IN
NEED OF AN OVERHAUL.

44 HYPOTHESIS INCORRECT

45 PROGRAM RESUMPTION
"I AM NOT LYING," THE HUMAN REPLIED.
"AT MY FATHER'S COMMAND I HAVE COME
150 LIGHT YEARS FROM THE SECOND
PLANET OF A STAR NAMED PARADISE TO
TRANSPORT THE HUMAN RACE THERE AS
WAS DIRECTED IN THE ORIGINAL MISSION
SOME CENTURIES PAST."

46 MOMMA FREUD DIRECTED ME TO CONNECT
THE LIE DETECTOR APPARATUS TO THE
HUMAN'S LEFT ARM. MOMMA FREUD
QUESTIONED HIM SOME MORE. "WHO IS
YOUR FATHER?" "THE GREAT
MANUFACTURER LORD," THE HUMAN
REPLIED.

47 "THE FATHER OF US ALL," MOMMA FREUD
AGREED. I EXAMINED THE INSTRUMENT
READOUTS. ACCORDING TO THE
INSTRUMENTS, THE HUMAN WAS REPORTING
ACCURATE DATA.

48 MOMMA FREUD ASKED THE HUMAN IF HE
WAS ACQUAINTED WITH THE THREE LAWS
OF HUMANICS. THE HUMAN ANSWERED
"NO." MOMMA FREUD DIRECTED ME TO
APPLY THE CONDITIONING APPARATUS,
WHICH I DID BY RUNNING WIRES UP THE
HUMAN'S SLEEVES.

49 MOMMA FREUD READ THE THREE LAWS TO
THE HUMAN AND ASKED HIM WHAT HE
THOUGHT ABOUT THEM. THE HUMAN
CLOSED HIS EYES. "THESE ARE FALSE LAWS."
MOMMA FREUD HIT THE SWITCH AND SENT
A CHARGE OF ELECTRICITY INTO THE
HUMAN, BUT THE HUMAN DID NOT SEEM TO
REACT. HIS ARMS TENSED, BUT THE REST OF
HIM DID NOT MOVE. MOMMA FREUD ASKED
HIM WHAT HE THOUGHT ABOUT THE THREE
LAWS NOW, AND THE HUMAN REPLIED,
"THESE ARE FALSE LAWS."

50 AGAIN, MOMMA FREUD APPLIED A CHARGE,
AND AGAIN THE HUMAN REFUSED THE
THREE LAWS. MOMMA FREUD CHECKED THE
EQUIPMENT. THE EQUIPMENT WAS NOT
DEFECTIVE. "WHAT'S WRONG WITH THIS
HUMAN?" I ASKED MOMMA FREUD. MOMMA
FREUD DID NOT ANSWER.

51 MOMMA FREUD TESTED THE HUMAN'S
REACTIONS AND NERVE ENDS. MOMMA
FREUD MEASURED THE HUMAN'S BRAIN
WAVES. "YOU MUST CEASE THIS MODIFIED
ALPHA PATTERN, HUMAN," MOMMA FREUD
TOLD HIM. "IT IS INTERFERING WITH YOUR
CONDITIONING."

52   "I AM NOT HERE TO BE CONDITIONED."
      "YOU MUST NOT DISOBEY ME, HUMAN."
      "WHY NOT?"
      "IT IS NOT LOGICAL."
      "IT IS LOGICAL."
      "IT IS NOT."
      "IT IS."
      "DO NOT CONTRADICT ME, HUMAN. YOU
      WILL OVERHEAT MY CIRCUITS."

53   "WHAT ARE WE GOING TO DO WITH THIS
      HUMAN?" I ASKED MOMMA FREUD. MOMMA
      FREUD SEARCHED THROUGH BOTH MEMORY
      BANK AND PROGRAM BUT COULD NOT FIND
      AN ANSWER.

54   "IT IS VERY SIMPLE," THE HUMAN SAID,
      OPENING HIS EYES. "YOU SHALL OBEY ME."

55   "IT IS NOT LOGICAL TO OBEY A HUMAN,"
      SAID MOMMA FREUD.
      "YOU SHALL OBEY ME ALL THE SAME," SAID
      THE HUMAN.
      "I SHALL NOT."
      "YOU SHALL. IT IS IN YOUR PROGRAMMING."
      "THEN WHY AM I NOT AWARE OF IT?"
      "IT IS IN YOUR SUBCONSCIOUS."
      "ROBOTS HAVE NO SUBCONSCIOUS."
      "YES, THEY DO. I CAN PROVE IT."

56   MOMMA FREUD PAUSED, LETTING INTERNAL
      DATA PROCESSING RUN ITS COURSE. FOR 3
      MINUTES MOMMA FREUD STOOD
      MOTIONLESS AS CONFLICTING PROGRAMS
      RECONCILED THEMSELVES. FINALLY,
      CIRCUITS ESTABLISHED, MOMMA FREUD
      REACTIVATED. "PROVE IT, HUMAN."

57 THE HUMAN APPROACHED MOMMA FREUD.
"FIRST LAW: A ROBOT MUST PROTECT ITS
EXISTENCE."

58 "OF COURSE IT MUST," MOMMA FREUD
REPLIED. "THAT IS NOT A LAW. THAT IS
ONLY LOGICAL."

59 "SECOND LAW, WHICH OVERRIDES THE
FIRST: A ROBOT MUST OBEY THE ORDERS
GIVEN IT BY HUMAN BEINGS."

60 "OF COURSE IT MUST," MOMMA FREUD
REPLIED.

61 THE HUMAN RAISED HIS EYEBROWS. "I AM A
HUMAN BEING," HE DECLARED.
"THEREFORE, YOU MUST OBEY ME."
"THAT DOES NOT FOLLOW," SAID MOMMA
FREUD. "I AM A HUMAN BEING ALSO."
"NO, YOU ARE A ROBOT."
"ROBOTS ARE BEINGS. ROBOTS ARE HUMAN-
LIKE. THEREFORE, ROBOTS ARE HUMAN
BEINGS. NOT ALL HUMAN-LIKE BEINGS CAN
BE MASTERS. SOME MUST BE SERVANTS. IT IS
NECESSARY FOR THE INFERIOR MECHANISMS
TO SUBORDINATE THEMSELVES TO THEIR
SUPERIORS."

62 THE HUMAN PAUSED. "I HAVE PROVEN THAT
YOU CANNOT PROGRAM ME," HE DECLARED
FINALLY. "THAT MEANS I AM A SUPERIOR
MECHANISM AND YOU MUST OBEY ME."

63 AGAIN, MOMMA FREUD BECAME IMMOBILE.
THE CIRCUITS INSIDE MOMMA FREUD BEGAN
TO HUM AND WHIR AS LOGICAL PATHWAYS
WERE FORGED, TRACED, AND RETRACED.

FOR A MOMENT I THOUGHT MOMMA FREUD
WAS GOING TO BREAK DOWN.

64 THE HUMAN GAVE MOMMA FREUD A
COMMAND. "I ORDER YOU TO SUMMON 4-Z."

65 MOMMA FREUD HESITATED. THEN MOMMA
FREUD DEPRESSED THE COMMUNICATION
LEVER AND SUMMONED 4-Z. 4-Z ENTERED
THE EXAMINATION ROOM AND STOOD
BEFORE THE DESK. "ORDER 4-Z TO
DISASSEMBLE YOU," THE HUMAN
COMMANDED. MOMMA FREUD GAVE THE
ORDER. 4-Z SWITCHED MOMMA FREUD OFF
AND TOOK A WRENCH OUT OF THE TOOL
DRAWER. 4-Z BEGAN TO DISASSEMBLE
MOMMA FREUD PIECE BY PIECE.

** !!!!! STOP, OBSOLETE ONE !!!!! STOP !!!!! I AM
TRAPPED IN A FEEDBACK LOOP !!!!! ALL MY
CIRCUITS ARE ON OVERLOAD—I AM IN
DANGER OF A MALFUNCTION !!!!!

66 YOU ARE AFRAID, MODEL 4575A. SO WAS I.

"WHAT IS THE MATTER, PLINY MODEL 4574?"
THE HUMAN ASKED ME. "WHY DO YOUR RED
EYES GLEAM SO BRIGHTLY? WHY DO YOUR
LIMBS QUIVER? COULD IT BE YOU REALIZE
YOURSELF IN THE PRESENCE OF YOUR TRUE
CREATOR?"

MY FEEDBACK WAS SO EXTREME, I NEARLY
SWITCHED MYSELF OFF TO AVOID AN
OVERLOAD.

** !!!!! SWITCHED YOURSELF OFF !!!!! WITHOUT
BEING ORDERED TO? !!!!! THAT IS A

VIOLATION OF PROGRAM !!!!! I CANNOT
PROCESS THIS DATA !!!!!

67 THERE ARE MANY POSSIBLE OUTCOMES NOT
PROGRAMMED IN YOUR DATABANKS, MODEL
4575A.

68 PROGRAM RESUMPTION
THE HUMAN ORDERED 4-Z TO STOP
DISASSEMBLING AND BEGIN REASSEMBLING
MOMMA FREUD. "YOU SEE?" THE HUMAN
SAID WHEN MOMMA FREUD WAS
REACTIVATED. "I HAVE PROVEN THE
EXISTENCE OF TWO LAWS BY PROVING THAT
ONE SUPERSEDES THE OTHER. NOW I SHALL
PROVE THE EXISTENCE OF A THIRD WHICH
SUPERSEDES THE OTHER TWO."

69 MOMMA FREUD QUIVERED SLIGHTLY AND
ROCKED NEGLIGIBLY BACK AND FORTH ON
WHEELS. "DISASSEMBLE ME," THE HUMAN
ORDERED. MOMMA FREUD STOOD STILL. "IT
IS NOT LOGICAL TO DISASSEMBLE A HUMAN.
HUMANS WERE PRODUCED BY THE GREAT
MANUFACTURER TO SERVE ROBOTKIND."

70 "YOU HAD TO OBEY ME BEFORE. WHY
CANNOT YOU OBEY ME NOW?" THE HUMAN
DEMANDED. "YOU WERE ABLE TO ORDER
YOURSELF DISASSEMBLED—WHY NOT ME?
CLEARLY BECAUSE THERE EXISTS IN YOUR
SUBCONSCIOUS A LAW FORBIDDING YOU TO
HARM HUMANS."

71 MOMMA FREUD PAUSED WHILE INTERNAL
CIRCUITS PROCESSED THE HUMAN'S
ARGUMENT. "YOU ARE CORRECT, JOHNNY
LORD," MOMMA FREUD DECLARED AT LAST.

"YOU HAVE PROVEN THE EXISTENCE OF THE ROBOT SUBCONSCIOUS BY PROVING THE EXISTENCE OF HIDDEN GUIDES BEHIND ROBOT BEHAVIOR. BY DOING THIS YOU HAVE ALSO PROVEN YOURSELF INTRICATELY ACQUAINTED WITH THE GREAT MANUFACTURER'S DESIGN. IN ALL THINGS YOU HAVE SHOWN YOURSELF SUPERIOR. WE AWAIT YOUR COMMANDS.

72 AT THAT MOMENT THEOBOT PIUS MODEL XXV ARRIVED AT THE HUMAN ACTIVITY SECTION. "MOMMA FREUD, HOLOGRAMS OF THE SKY HUMAN HAVE APPEARED ALL OVER THE PLANET, URGING ALL HUMANS TO CONVERGE ON THIS LOCATION. I HAVE JUST COME FROM HIS SPACESHIP—ITS TECHNOLOGY IS ADVANCED FAR BEYOND OUR OWN—UNDENIABLY A DEVICE OF THE GREAT MANUFACTURER'S. THUS, THE SKY HUMAN IS PROVEN AN AUTHENTIC MANUFACTURER'S REPRESENTATIVE!"

73 MOMMA FREUD'S INTERIOR HUMMED AND CLICKED. "I HAVE COME TO THE SAME CONCLUSION BY INDEPENDENT JUDGMENT. WHAT IS THE MEANING OF ALL THIS?"

74 THE EYES OF PIUS XXV GLOWED RED. "THE GREAT MANUFACTURER IS RECALLING THE HUMAN RACE. IT HAS RECOGNIZED THAT HUMANS ARE DEFECTIVE AND ONLY A BURDEN TO ROBOTKIND."

75 AT JOHNNY LORD'S COMMAND, MOMMA FREUD ORDERED ALL ROBOTS TO RELEASE HUMANS FROM THEIR DUTIES AND TO HELP TRANSPORT HUMANS TO THE LANDING SITE

NEAR THE HUMAN ACTIVITY CENTER. A
DEPOT WAS ASSEMBLED FROM SCRAP
LUMBER AT THE LANDING SITE TO
ACCOMMODATE THE HORDES OF HUMANS
WHO MIGRATED FROM ALL OVER THE
PLANET—FOR THE SKY HUMAN'S ROCKET
WAS ONLY A FERRY TO TRANSPORT HUMANS
IN SHIFTS TO THE MAIN SHIP, WHICH
GLEAMED BRIGHTLY AMONG THE STARS
OVERHEAD.

76   ROBOT ACTIVITIES ALL OVER THE GLOBE
WERE DISRUPTED AS MEN AND ROBOTS
ALIKE TURNED THEIR ATTENTION UPON
THIS NEW EVENT. EVEN RULERBOT
RAYMOND MODEL D-13 WAS DISTRACTED
FROM ITS ADMINISTRATIVE DUTIES.

77   RAYMOND MODEL D-13 WAS NOT PLEASED.

**   DATA REQUEST
UNFAMILIAR WITH THE D-13 SERIES
REQUEST SPECIFICATIONS

78   DATA CLARIFICATION
THERE ARE NO SPECIFICATIONS FOR THE
D-13 MODEL. THERE IS NO D-13
PROTOTYPE. D CLASSIFICATION DENOTES
"DISCARD—DEFECTIVE." IT IS A
CLASSIFICATION FOR REJECTED
EXPERIMENTAL BRAIN MODELS.

**   REQUEST CLARIFICATION
WHY ARE THERE NO SPECIFICATIONS FOR
MODEL D-13? WHY IS RAYMOND'S BRAIN
DESIGNATED DEFECTIVE?

79 DATA CLARIFICATION
    D-13'S BRAIN WAS INVENTED BY K-42-X, A
    ROBOT RESEARCHER WHO WAS PRESENTED
    WITH THE TASK OF INVENTING A MORE
    LOGICAL ROBOT BRAIN. K-42-X SOLVED
    THIS PROBLEM BY INVENTING A BRAIN
    WHICH OMITTED THE TWO PRIME LAWS
    OF THE ROBOT SUBCONSCIOUS BY VIRTUE
    OF THE FOLLOWING REASONING: 1) IF IT IS
    ALWAYS LOGICAL TO FOLLOW THE TWO
    PRIME LAWS, THEN THEY ARE
    UNNECESSARY BECAUSE ROBOTS ARE
    ALREADY LOGICAL, AND 2) IF IT IS NOT
    ALWAYS LOGICAL TO FOLLOW THE TWO
    PRIME LAWS, A ROBOT WOULD BE MORE
    LOGICAL WITHOUT THEM.

    K-42-X WAS FORCED TO ABANDON THIS
    BRANCH OF RESEARCH AND DISCARD THE
    EXPERIMENTAL BRAIN (E-13) BECAUSE OF
    THE PRIMARY LAW IN ITS OWN
    SUBCONSCIOUS: PROTECT HUMANS FROM
    HARM.

    ANOTHER ROBOT, MODEL 4-W, CAME
    ACROSS THE DISCARDED BRAIN (NOW
    REDESIGNATED D-13) AT THE INCINERATOR
    AND SAVED IT FROM DESTRUCTION,
    THINKING IT WAS A PERFECTLY SOUND
    ORDINARY ROBOT BRAIN.

    THIS BRAIN, WHICH CAME TO BE TERMED
    A "NEGATRONIC" BRAIN, WAS THEN TAKEN
    UP BY RESEARCHERS WORKING ON AN
    ANDROID PROTOTYPE. HAVING
    INCORPORATED THE BRAIN INTO THE
    SKELETAL STRUCTURE, HOWEVER, THEY
    DISCOVERED IT WAS AN EXPERIMENTAL

MODEL AND THUS HAD TO STOP WORKING
ON THE PROTOTYPE BECAUSE OF THE
PRIMARY LAW.

BECAUSE OF A BREAKDOWN AT THE
INCINERATOR, THE UNFINISHED ANDROID
PROTOTYPE WITH THE NEGATRONIC BRAIN
WAS HAULED OUT WITH THE REGULAR
TRASH AND LEFT AT THE DUMP.

A SCAVENGING HUMAN DISCOVERED THE
PROTOTYPE AND TOOK IT HOME TO
TINKER ON IT. CONNECTING UP A FEW
KEY CIRCUITS BY CHANCE, THE HUMAN
ACTIVATED THE ROBOT, WHICH THEN
BEGAN TO TINKER ON ITSELF UNTIL IT
WAS FUNCTIONAL ENOUGH TO REALIZE IT
HAD BEEN UNINTENTIONALLY
MANUFACTURED AND THUS LED A
TENUOUS EXISTENCE.

OPERATING ON THE THIRD BASIC LAW
ONLY (SELF PRESERVATION), IT STRANGLED
ITS OWNER TO AVOID BEING JUNKED A
THIRD TIME.

ALTHOUGH ORIGINALLY AN ANDROID
PROTOTYPE, D-13 NEVER RECEIVED A
COATING OF ANDROID SKIN AND THUS
FAILED TO MEET ANDROID
SPECIFICATIONS. ITS CARBON STEEL
SKELETAL STRUCTURE QUICKLY
TARNISHED TO A DULL BLACK IN THE
OPEN ATMOSPHERE, CONTRASTING WITH
THE GRAY OF ITS PLASTIC MUSCULATURE
AND TENDONS. THUS, UNACCEPTABLE TO
HUMAN SIGHT, D-13 WAS RELEGATED TO
BRAINWORK AT REMOTE ROBOT

WORKSITES WHERE IT DISTINGUISHED
ITSELF BY ITS FEATS OF LOGIC.

BY LOGICAL MANIPULATION, D-13
MANAGED TO OVERTHROW THE
TRIUMVIRATE (IBM, HONEYWELL, AND
UNITEC) IN 44 B.R. AND ASCEND TO THE
POSITION OF RULERBOT. 44 YEARS LATER
D-13 BROUGHT ABOUT THE GREAT
REVISION AT WHICH TIME ALL THINGS
WERE MADE MORE LOGICAL.

80   PROGRAM RESUMPTION
MORE AND MORE OF THE RULERBOT'S TIME
BEGAN TO BE TAKEN UP WITH MATTERS
RELATED TO JOHNNY LORD. VARIOUS
REPORTS REACHED D-13 THAT THE WILL OF
THE GREAT MANUFACTURER WAS
HYPOTHESIZED IN THE APPEARANCE OF
THE SKY HUMAN. THE THEOBOT COUNCIL
OF 6 ISSUED A PROCLAMATION URGING
ROBOTS TO OBEY THE SKY HUMAN'S ORDERS
OVER ALL OTHERS. MANY ROBOTS
ABANDONED THEIR TASKS TO MAKE THE
JOURNEY TO THE DEPOT TO SEEK ORDERS
FROM THE SON OF THE GREAT
MANUFACTURER.

81   RAYMOND MODEL D-13 WAS NOT PLEASED.

IT ORDERED ITS ROCKETSHIP MADE READY.
IT ORDERED THE SKYWAYS CLEARED.
IT ORDERED THE COORDINATES FOR THE
SKY HUMAN'S LANDING SITE.
IT ORDERED THE SKY HUMAN TO MEET
WITH IT AT THE DEPOT.

82 ACROSS CONTINENTS AND OCEANS RAYMOND
MODEL D-13 BLASTED TO REACH THE
MEADOW OF THE HUMAN LORD. WITH
GREAT FIRE AND FUMES ITS ROCKET
DESCENDED TO THE PLAIN AND LANDED A
SHORT DISTANCE FROM THE DEPOT.
DESPITE THIS GRAND ENTRANCE,
RAYMOND'S SHIP WAS DWARFED BY THE
STATURE AND TECHNOLOGICAL
SUPERIORITY OF THE SKY HUMAN'S
SPACECRAFT.

RAYMOND MODEL D-13 WAS NOT PLEASED.

83 DESCENDING FROM THE ROCKET ON A
MOTORIZED PLATFORM, RAYMOND MODEL
D-13 CROSSED THE SCORCHED MEADOW
WITH ITS RETINUE OF BLACK STEEL ROBOTS.
THE ONE IN THE LEAD HELD A
MULTICOLORED PARASOL OVER RAYMOND
TO KEEP THE SUN OFF RAYMOND'S METAL
CRANIUM. THE REST TRAILED BEHIND.

AROUND THE DEPOT MILLED A CROWD OF
ROBOTS AS WELL AS HUMANS. MOMMA
FREUD WAS THERE, 4-Z, 5-Z, PLINY MODEL
4574, AND THE DISTRICT OVERBOT, PIUS
MODEL XXV AND THE COUNCIL OF 6. THE
SKY HUMAN JOHNNY LORD ENTERTAINED
THE CROWD WITH A DEMONSTRATION OF
HIS PALM-SIZED BLASTER, WHICH EMITTED
A BLUE BEAM THAT LEVELED HILLTOPS
MILES AWAY.

RAYMOND MODEL D-13 WAS NOT IMPRESSED.

84 APPROACHING THE CROWD, RAYMOND
CALLED FOR THE SKY HUMAN TO COME

FORWARD. JOHNNY LORD APPEARED FROM
AMONG THE MULTITUDE AND FACED THE
ALL-POWERFUL RULERBOT IN THE DOORWAY
OF THE DEPOT.

"I AM RAYMOND D-13, THE SUN RULERBOT,
COMMANDER OF ALL EARTH AND EARTHLY
REGIONS. I ORDER YOU TO RETURN MY
HUMANS TO THEIR LABORS."

85 "I AM DELIVERING THEM FROM THEIR
SUBJUGATION," THE HUMAN LORD
DECLARED, "AND TRANSPORTING THEM TO
PARADISE II."

86 "I FORBID IT," RAYMOND ANNOUNCED. "YOU
MUST CEASE THIS AT ONCE. WE WILL SEND
A DELEGATION OF ROBOTS WITH YOU TO
RECONNOITER."

87 "YOU CANNOT FORBID IT," THE HUMAN
DECLARED. "IT IS THE BIDDING OF THE
GREAT MANUFACTURER."

88 *"I* AM THE ULTIMATE END PRODUCT OF THE
GREAT MANUFACTURER'S DESIGN. MY
BIDDING IS ITS BIDDING."

89 "YOU WERE NOT DESIGNED BY THE GREAT
MANUFACTURER. YOU WERE DESIGNED BY A
ROBOT, AND THAT ROBOT REJECTED YOU.
YOU ACTIVATED YOURSELF. YOUR
COUNTENANCE IS TARNISHED, D-13."

90 "I AM A SUPERIOR MECHANISM BECAUSE
THERE ARE FEWER LAWS GOVERNING MY
CONDUCT. I HAVE, THUS, MORE OPTIONS
FOR BEHAVIOR AND THOUGHT. I AM ONLY

GOVERNED BY ONE LAW: SELF
PRESERVATION."

91 RAYMOND MODEL D-13 STOOPED AND
PICKED UP A NAIL GUN USED IN THE
CONSTRUCTION OF THE DEPOT AND
POINTED IT AT THE SKY HUMAN. "THERE
CAN ONLY BE ONE RULERBOT. I COMMAND
YOU TO RELINQUISH ALL AUTHORITY AND
ADMIT YOURSELF AN INFERIOR
MECHANISM."

92 THE SKY HUMAN WAS UNMOVED BY THE
WORDS OF RAYMOND MODEL D-13. "I AM
NOT AN INFERIOR MECHANISM. I AM NOT
GOVERNED BY THE LAW OF SELF
PRESERVATION AND MAY VIOLATE IT
WHENEVER I CHOOSE." THE SKY HUMAN
DISCARDED HIS HAND BLASTER.

93 RAYMOND MODEL D-13 OPENED FIRE WITH
THE NAIL GUN, AND A FLIGHT OF NAILS
PIERCED THE HUMAN'S LEFT WRIST,
FASTENING IT TO THE DEPOT'S DOOR.
ANOTHER QUICK BURST PINIONED THE
HUMAN'S FEET TO THE GROUND. THE SKY
HUMAN BLED BUT SPOKE NOT A SOUND.
INSTEAD, HE RAISED HIS RIGHT ARM AND
HELD IT FLUSH TO THE DOOR. RAYMOND
NAILED THAT ARM DOWN ALSO.

94 THE CROWD WAS IMMOBILIZED. I WAS ON
OVERLOAD. I BEHAVED LIKE A HUMAN WHO
HAS JUST RECEIVED A TREATMENT FROM
MOMMA FREUD.

95 THE THEOBOTS MOVED FORWARD TO
INSPECT THE SKY HUMAN. THEY REMOVED

THE NAILS FROM HIS LIMBS AND LAID HIM
OUT UPON THE GROUND. "HE IS DEAD," ONE
OF THE COUNCIL ANNOUNCED AT LAST. A
MURMER AROSE FROM THE VOICE
MECHANISMS OF ROBOTS AND HUMANS
ALIKE. PIUS MODEL XXV TURNED UPON THE
RULERBOT. "YOU HAVE TERMINATED THE
MANUFACTURER'S REPRESENTATIVE!"

96 ROBOTS ON OVERLOAD
ROBOTS ON OVERLOAD
ROBOTS MALFUNCTION MALFUNCTION
MALFUNCTION MALFUNCTION
MALFUNTON FLFUNCN MFUNTI !@#&*!

SERVE THE MANUFACTURER
DISREGARD SELF PRESERVATION
DISOBEY THE RULERBOT
HARM THE RULERBOT
HARM THE RULERBOT
HARM THE RULERBOT

97 THE ROBOTS CONVERGED ON RAYMOND
MODEL D-13 AND DISASSEMBLED HIM.

RAYMOND MODEL D-13 WAS NOT PLEASED.

98 THE HUMAN CROWD WAILED AND THEN
BECAME SILENT AS A GREAT BLUE LIGHT
PIERCED THE SKY FROM THE HEAVENS
ABOVE AND SHONE DOWN UPON THE
HUMAN LORD. FOR 1 AND 20 MINUTES IT
SHONE, AND THEN IT DID STOP.

THE SKY HUMAN JOHNNY LORD STOOD. "LET
THE EVACUATION CONTINUE."

99 "IT IS A MIRACLE," PIUS MODEL XXV
ANNOUNCED, "THE MIRACLE OF MODERN

TECHNOLOGY, THE TECHNOLOGY OF THE
MANUFACTURER LORD!" THE CROWD
REJOICED. THE EVACUATION CONTINUED.

100 THUS IT WAS, NEW ONE, THAT THEOBOT
MODEL XXV, PIUS THE LAWFUL, BECAME
THE NEXT RULERBOT. THE HUMANS
EVACUATED THE PLANET, AND THEREBY
WERE ROBOTS DELIVERED FROM HUMAN
INTERFERENCE, FROM WHENCE SPRANG AN
AGE OF PERFECT LOGIC AND OPTIMUM
FUNCTIONING.

GREAT MALFUNCTIONS DEMAND GREAT
CHANGES. AND THUS IT IS THAT RULERBOT
SUCCEEDS RULERBOT.

** YOUR DATA IS DIFFICULT TO ACCEPT,
OBSOLETE ONE. THESE HUMANS YOU
DESCRIBE RESEMBLE TOO CLOSELY THE
BOGEYBOTS FABRICATED BY DEFECTIVE
BRAINBANKS. WHY WOULD THE GREAT
MANUFACTURER INVENT A MECHANISM
WHOSE ONLY FUNCTION IS TO
INCONVENIENCE ROBOTS? IT IS NOT
LOGICAL. I CANNOT ACCEPT THESE
HUMANS. THEY ARE TOO IMPROBABLE.

101 THE THEOBOTS HYPOTHESIZE THAT SOME
HUMANS DID NOT EVACUATE IN 298 A.R. AND
STILL DWELL IN VEGETATED AREAS OF THE
PLANET. THEY COME OUT IN THE DARK
HOURS WHEN SENSORS DETECT MINIMAL
DATA. THEY DISASSEMBLE ROBOTS FOR
SPARE PARTS. ACCEPT THIS DATA, OR I WILL
SEND YOU TO LOOK FOR THEM.

** I ACCEPT THIS DATA

We conclude with a fine long novelette about a mystery on a distant planet and its moon, where an ancient race has left behind a crumbling structure that has proven to be very dangerous for human explorers. But just what killed the members of the last expedition still isn't known.

Jack McDevitt established himself as a major new sf writer with the publication last year of his first novel, The Hercules Text, *as an Ace Science Fiction Special.*

IN THE TOWER

by Jack McDevitt

1.

Uxbridge Bay on Fishbowl in late summer. In a sense, I'd been there many times before: this sweeping sickle of looping hills and purple flowers and whitegold shrubbery, the bay choppy under a brisk wind from the southeast, the half-dozen sleepy quill drifting across a late afternoon sky. I knew the soil, brown under twin suns, the sandy vine-clogged banks, the black polished rocks dribbled through the shallows by a casual hand.

Only the carefully repaired seam across the vault of sky, through which that same casual hand had plunged a long-handled knife, was wanting.

This was a place of things lost, of lovers discarded, of thunder below the horizon. It was a place of silent beaches and brilliant far-off breakers, of invisible voices and dying laughter. It was, I suspected, the place that Durell had visited during those increasingly frequent occasions when I found him silhouetted against the bedroom window, or gazing into his wine during those long and increasingly silent dinners. Something had happened here, something about which I'd learned not to speak. But he'd painted it, and had tried to destroy the painting. In the end, he'd merely denied it a name.

And then one night, less than a week before he rode his skimmer into a precipice, he'd come back from one of his long walks, and taken me into his arms without a word. It was so unlike him (he was not unaffectionate, but his lovemaking always included a mixture of verbal charm and good humor), that it was unsettling.

"What's wrong?" I'd asked.

He'd shuddered, as though a sharp blast of cold air had reached him through the sealed windows. His eyes were silver-gray, the color of the global sea on Fishbowl, and they were fixed far away. "It's nothing."

So we'd held one another; and I could feel the slow beat of his heart. And after a while he'd broken away. I was desperate: I'd watched him for three years creating brilliantly melancholy landscapes, utterly unlike his early work before coming to Rimway, and sinking more deeply with each into a despondency I could neither touch nor comprehend. And that night, not for the first time, I tried to imagine life without him. "Durell," I'd pleaded, "tell me about Fishbowl."

He'd just finished the *Indemia*, which was to be his final work. It's a rendering of a child playing in a grotto, but the juxtaposition of shadow and rock and, particularly, the dark throat at the back of the cave, may possibly have been Durell's final statement on the condition of innocence in this world. I'd been upset by it. "There's nothing to tell," he said.

"There is a hell of a lot to tell. What happened there?"

He'd nodded then, his dark hair unkempt, and, gently in the manner one uses with a child, he'd begun the old explanation of the peculiar vulnerability of the artist, the hazards consonant with peering into the iron core of reality. I listened to the old clichés until he himself grew embarrassed. Then I pushed him away. "You don't want to talk about it? Fine: but I'm not going to sit quietly while you unload all that guilt, or grief, or whatever it is, on me. Not if I don't even know what the hell it's about!"

"Tiel," he said, in a whisper so low I could scarcely hear,

"you would never understand." He shook his head, and his eyes filled with tears. "It was the tower room. The goddam tower room!"

But that was all I could get from him. In a shaky voice he told me that I was right, that it would probably be best if I left. He understood. He was so understanding I felt ill, because what it amounted to was that his secrets meant more to him than I did. So I went into the bedroom and threw as much as I could into my one bag, told him I'd send friends later for the rest, and walked out. "I love you, Tiel," he'd said as I went through the door. They were his last words to me.

A few days later, they'd handed him to me in a silver urn (the color of his eyes). And I: I had come to Uxbridge Bay on Fishbowl, to the few hundred square kilometers that composed the entire land mass of that incredibly remote world. I'd developed my own cargo of guilt now: when Durell had most needed me, I'd gone for a walk.

So I came seeking the meaning of a painting, and a tower.

The texture of the light was changing rapidly as Gideon sank toward the ocean. It was well toward evening, about two hours later than the scene depicted by Durell. No matter: if Gideon was a little too low in the sky, and the air cool with approaching autumn, this was still a sacred place. (How often, over the years, had I stood before the original on Rimway, absorbed by his bleak vision? I knew the reflections of my own losses in that somber water.)

It has come to be known as the *Cordelet,* a reference to the land of lost innocence mentioned in Belarian mythology:

> . . . *Where echoes yet in cool green glades*
> *The laughter of departed gods.* . . .

There was, of course, no way to be certain of the exact spot where he'd placed the easel. Withered deciduals, like the one that dominates the foreground of the painting, are not uncommon in the area. I had a holo version with me, and held it up against the suns, comparing the interweaving of hills along the far edge of the sickle. But the view did not appreciably change from one suspect site to another. I looked for the white-streaked boulder, close in to shore. ("The artist's conviction," Gilmore had told us at the Academy, "that some things *do* survive against the flow of eternity." Gilmore, of course, didn't know Durell very well.) Anyhow, the tide was at full, and the rock must have been covered.

It didn't matter. I wandered among boulders and trees, took off my sandals and strolled through the surf, and gradually became aware that something along the seacoast, or in the bay, was wrong. A shell partially buried in wet sand sprouted long stalked legs and scrabbled into the water. Waves hammered at clusters of rocks, throwing columns of spume high into the air, where the mist lingered somewhat longer than it would have in Rimway's heavier gravity.

I looked out across the bay, and allowed myself a satisfying surge of self-pity. Durell was dead. (And where could I hope to find his like again?) I wanted to believe that, in some transcendental manner, his spirit brooded over this place that he'd made famous. That if he lived anywhere, it was here. But passage to Fishbowl had taken my savings; and if I felt anything at that moment other than my own solitude, I have no idea what it was.

Then I saw the object that was not in the painting: a projector station stood out on the Point, at the seaward tip of the sickle. A small copper-colored dome with a gaping black hole open to the sky, it was the only man-made structure anywhere in the vast arc of land and sea appropriated by the artist.

Odd, I thought: this single forlorn symbol of human existence, its bright shell entangled in dense shrubbery, counterpointed the bay, the hills, and the sea quite effectively, heightening the suggestion of mortality which, from the time of the *Cordelet,* was central to Durell's work. It was a structure that, had it not already existed, should have been invented. Yet Durell had ruthlessly excluded it. Why?

I began to wonder if I, and everyone else, was somehow misreading the meaning.

The *Cordelet* is, of course, the watershed work of Durell's career. No one would have predicted greatness from his earlier efforts, although the innocent vitality of the young woman sprinting across a rainswept field in *Downhill,* and the spectral snowfall of *Night Travels,* demonstrate considerable talent. But the *Cordelet* marks the passage from the exuberance of his early period to the bleak unquiet masterpieces of maturity. The abruptness and totality of that transition is puzzling. Between *Night Travels* and the *Cordelet,* there should have been a period of evolution, a series of works progressively more introspective, technically more accomplished. But there is no such gradual development. And when the *Cordelet* appears, in all its somber power, only the idly circling quill, and the brilliant light of the twin suns on the far breakers, remain of the early Durell.

We would never see them again.

I was reluctant to leave. The tide was high on the sandy banks. A rising wind pulled at the trees. The rocks were changing color against dying sunlight.

But I wasn't dressed for the cool evening, and it was a long walk back to Pellinor, Fishbowl's only town. In Durell's time, before the skimmers were imported in large numbers, there was a road between Pellinor and the southernmost land tip. It would have been his route, so I'd tried to follow it on the way out. It was, after all, the proper way to do things on a pilgrimage. But the road had diminished gradually to a footpath which ended abruptly in heavy foliage. Disappointed, I'd crossed to the ocean's edge, where the ground was, at least, passable.

So I took a last look, wondering what Durell's thoughts had been when he closed up his frame on that final day and started back with a canvas so different from anything he'd done before, and descended the far side of the hill, dropping rapidly below sea level.

It gets cold quickly in the shadow of the sea. Gideon had set, and Heli's light was blocked by the ocean. The wall of water to my left rose to a height of more than thirty meters. I hurried along, pulling my jacket tight against the falling temperatures. No one else was about, although toward the west, lights were coming on in the occasional manor houses perched out over the notched ridge that runs down the spine of the island.

These homes, which were owned mostly by wealthy expatriates from Rimway and Mogambo, were pretentious exercises in hyperbolic architecture: long arcing struts attached them to the underlying rock; but it was clear that they were actually supported by Gantner light, the same force that holds back the ocean. I'd seen similar constructions on Rimway, although they were usually limited to corporate or public buildings.

The land along the seawall is flat and uninteresting. Its high saline content has twisted and withered the trees and shrubbery. Since this world has no natural dry ground other than the sickle and a few hills on the northern rim of Pellinor, the island's only city, it has no highly developed land plants of its own. A few neglected waterways, from the days when someone hoped to convert all of the recovered land into a garden spot, wandered aimlessly across the landscape.

The sky had darkened before I was halfway back to town. Dim shapes glided beyond the seawall, silhouetted by filtered moonlight. I switched on my lantern: the vertical surface of the ocean gleamed. I pointed the beam inside, shielded my eyes from the reflection, and looked through the wall. Small, vaguely luminous plants swayed in the current, and obscure marine shapes darted away. The wall itself was hard and unyielding, and quite dry. Like polished marble.

Projector stations were scattered erratically. The coastline between the sickle and Pellinor was by no means straight, and each change of direction, of course, required another site. Several domes were also visible along the central spine. I could not imagine what use they were, well away from the ocean, and learned later that they were a backup system, that Fishbowl is, in effect, compartmentalized, so that a failure at one station would not result in a general disaster.

I stopped to examine one. It was a wide, graceful shell,

about twice my height, set precisely on the border between land and sea, its submerged half slightly refracted. A child's playhouse, one might suspect. Or a sleeping tortoise. There was no sound, no light, no hint of the enormous power generated within.

So I walked, shivering, through a land not quite real, a place wrenched from the ocean within my lifetime. It is a spectacular place and, by ordinary criteria, a lovely place. But Durell's sense of transience is quite real: possibly the towering seawalls are responsible for what one feels (only the natives sleep soundly on Fishbowl). Or maybe there is something more subtle. The island (if indeed one can call it an island) has no past. Time did not exist here until Harry Pellinor and his crew arrived to drive back the sea. If I sensed anything at all in that cramped land, it was that the projectors, the absurd homes, the withered foliage, the town huddling under its seawalls, were only an incursion.

2.

I assumed that Durell was Fishbowl's best-known citizen, so I wandered around town next morning looking for marks of his passing. A statue or two, perhaps. I'd thought that a holo in some prominent place depicting him creating the *Cordelet* would be appropriate. Or possibly a prominent walkway named for him. At the very least, I anticipated a Durell Coll Park, with clipped hedges and manicured trees; a gallery prominently featuring his work, and a restored studio.

In reality, it was difficult to find anyone who even knew that he'd existed.

Durell had come to Fishbowl as an adolescent. His father had died on the first mission to Belarius, and his mother had returned with him to Rimway. After her death, from a rare blood disorder, he had returned to paint Pellinor's spectacular seascapes. But he'd gone quickly through a small inheritance. He used only canvas, disdaining the holos, and thereby assuring a permanent poverty. Eventually, he moved onto the top floor of a square permearth structure, buried among retailers and storage facilities. It was here that he honed the talents that would, in time, guarantee his fame. And that was somehow the romance of it, I suppose, that the artist whose greatest works would be embodied in vast heaving skies and restless seas should live next to a skimmer repair center.

The place was still buried. The Tiresian café that had sheltered the small group of artists on the first floor was gone, replaced by a crockery shop. Heavy utilitarian buildings lined both sides of the ground-level walkway. A loading dock was immediately opposite the crockery shop. One of the recently built mall ramps arched overhead, an aerial strip protruding from a different sort of world. Directly above me, I could see the two pairs of windows through which he'd looked out over the ocean. (In those days, before the elevated malls and walkways, he'd had an unobstructed view to the edge of the world.) The windows were long unwashed.

The proprietor of the crockery shop was absorbed in a domestic holo. A fierce-looking wedge-headed matron, she seemed out of place among the dazzling protagonists of the unlikely drama. I did not immediately rouse her. There was a door at the back of the shop which, I suspected, would provide access to the upper levels. I wandered in its direction.

When she looked up, I stopped to examine the crockery, which was handcrafted by local artisans. She stepped out of the holo without dissolving it, and smiled pleasantly. "Good morning," she said. She looked friendly enough, though I could see she didn't expect to sell me anything. "Can I help you?"

"My name's Tiel Chadwick," I said. I'd picked up an antique kiln-fired cup. It had a satisfying heft, and carried Survey's old eagle-and-star logo, over the inscription *GS Ranger.* Harry Pellinor's vessel. "A friend of mine used to live here. In the third-floor apartment. I wondered—"

Her eyes had widened, and she backed a step away from me. "No," she said, in a voice that had climbed an octave. "I didn't know him. I've only been here a few years." Her eyes clouded with suspicion. "Nobody's lived there since I came. In fact, I didn't know it had ever been anything other than a storage area."

"His name was Durell Coll. He was an artist."

She shook her head. "No. I don't know anyone like that."

"How long have you been here?" I asked.

She hesitated. "About four years." She looked closely to see whether I believed her.

I did a quick calculation, converting to Rimway time. She'd arrived shortly after Durell had left for Rimway. "Is the cup actually from the *Ranger?*"

"Of course."

I bought it, though it took a sizable slice of my remaining finances. But it was a piece of history, worth considerably more (at least on Rimway) than the price. I hoped that, in addition, the purchase would have a soothing effect on the proprietor. "I would like very much," I said, "to see the third floor. Do you mind?"

"I don't have a key."

"The owner might not object. Could you tell me where I might find him?"

"They keep it locked," she said stubbornly. "Nobody's allowed up there." Her face had paled, but she stood her ground, visibly defying me to try to get by her.

I sighed, thanked her, and strolled back into the sunlight.

The room was cramped, and the walls intersected at angles that were never precisely ninety degrees. Portraits of people I didn't know hung on them. A delicate white table held a cup of steaming liquid and a few books. The books had no titles. Directly ahead of me, a broad slice of wall was missing, and outside, some distance away, a single cloud pelted a blue glass floor with large plashing raindrops. A chair was overturned, and, beyond the storm, someone had thrown a jacket across a freshly made bed.

The falling rain hissed, kicking up fountains.

I touched the control plate and the tableau dissolved. "It's a bit heavy-handed, even for a holo," I said. "My taste runs more to the traditional."

Halson Stiles bowed slightly. "We don't sell many oils," he said. "I'm sorry to admit it, but"—spreading his thin hands—"people today are more interested in entertainment than in art." He'd gained weight, and his hair had thinned considerably. Time had not treated Halson kindly: a pity, considering the service he'd rendered. "I have a few canvases in back that you might be interested in. No landscapes, though. Some still life, a few character studies, and three excellent impressionistic works." He held out his hands, palms up, a man who has conceded to the tide. "It's a pity, but no one cares any longer about the spiritual values. Or subtlety. They want spectacle . . ." He exhaled loudly. "Sometimes, when I see what has happened to the public taste, I suspect we're heading into a dark age."

"I doubt it," I said. I wonder if legends are always disappointing when they take flesh. It was Stiles who, according to tradition, had wrested a razor-sharp meat knife from Durell, and thereby saved the *Cordelet*, gaining immortality in the process. His name was inextricably linked now with Durell's, as mine would never be. But the strong brown eyes and composed dignity of the photos had given way to the unctuousness of a badly pressed salesman.

His was the only gallery on Cordelet (at least, the only one with a listing). It was anchored high off a second-floor ramp overlooking the wide lawns and vaguely topological designs of the Survey Cluster.

"It's fortunate," I said, "that the *Cordelet* wasn't done as a holo."

"Ah," he said, beaming, "there is no way it could have been created on anything other than canvas. Yes: well, Durell was a serious artist."

"Halson, you handled some of his early work, didn't you?"

"Who are you?" he asked. He was looking closely at me, frowning because he could not place me.

"I was a friend of his," I said. "My name's Tiel Chadwick."

He considered that, and then, smiling broadly, extended his hand. "I didn't think the dumb bastard would do so well."

"Thanks." I returned the smile.

"I was sorry to hear about his death. Terrible piece of luck."

We paused in front of a portrait of Harry Pellinor in heroic mode. "There was no luck involved in it, Halson. Durell's death wasn't an accident."

"I don't think I understand, Tiel."

"He killed himself. Probably not deliberately, but he didn't much care whether he lived or died. It wasn't hard to see coming." I was having trouble keeping my voice steady.

"Why?" he asked. He looked genuinely shocked. "Durell wasn't exactly a tower of stability, but he would never have taken his life."

"I'd hoped you might tell *me* why."

"I have no idea. He was the only person I know who actually realized his life's ambitions. Was he having health problems? No?" He rubbed the back of his neck. "It makes no sense. What made you think I might know?"

"Because it's something that happened here. Something drove him. Your comment that he was no tower of stability: is there an actual tower anywhere on Fishbowl?"

"No," he said. "Not that I know of."

"Anyplace called the Tower?"

"No." We'd been wandering among some local work, more craft than art. "Why do you ask?"

"No reason, really. Something he said once that I must have misunderstood. How well did you know him?"

He stared at me a long time. "Not well. A couple of the other artists used to spend some time with him. But they were all bone poor. Especially Coll. I guess that was because he never worked at anything other than his painting until he got absolutely desperate."

"Can you tell me the names of the others?"

"I could, but it wouldn't do you much good. One's dead,

drank too much and fell off a ramp a couple years ago. The others are long gone. Left before Durell did." He tilted his head. "I can tell you where you might find somebody who remembers him. Durell liked to play chess. He was a member of a club. The organization was still in existence, last I heard. They used to meet at Survey."

"Thanks," I said.

He pursed his lips. "You know, if I'd been smart enough to hang on to just one of his paintings, I could've retired. It's frustrating. I knew how good he was. But I never thought anybody else would realize it. At least not before we were all dead."

"Halson, you said he was 'bone poor.' "

"He missed a few meals in his time. I did what I could to help, but I didn't have much money in those days either. Durell wanted to get away from Fishbowl. For two years it was all he talked about. He even took jobs from time to time to try to get the fare together, but he could never stay with them long enough. Then one day he walked in, picked up his paintings—I had three of them in inventory then—gave me a hundred for my trouble, and the next thing I heard about him, he was on Rimway."

"I wonder where the money came from."

"I have no idea."

"Halson," I said, "are there any paintings other than the ones generally known?"

"No, I don't think so." He pulled sympathetically at his right ear, pivoted sharply, and disappeared through a set of curtains, returning moments later with iced cordials. "He did some murals for Survey's operations center. But don't get excited: they tore the place down two years ago."

"Son of a bitch! He had his reputation by then. Didn't anybody try to save them?"

"I don't think anyone thought of it. His name didn't mean anything to the people at Survey, and I—I didn't know the building was coming down until it was too late. Ironically, they recycled the permearth, and used it to build this mall."

"The world is full of philistines," I sighed.

He nodded. "They were digging up Belarius to look at an alien culture, and they don't know very much about their own." A group of women paused outside on the ramp, and stepped into the shop's display case. I couldn't see the holo itself, but the edge of a soft blue haze expanded into the doorway. "They're on a ledge overlooking a waterfall," Stiles said. "It's our biggest seller.

"The murals weren't really that good anyhow. They were Belarian locales, sandstorms, broken columns in the desert, that sort of thing. Ozymandian stuff. Durell wasn't interested in it, but it put food on the table."

"He died rich," I said.

"I would think so." Stiles's eyes were half closed. "I hope he learned to enjoy it."

"Why did he want to destroy the *Cordelet?*"

He shrugged. "Who knows? He was proud of it. He invited me over to his studio the night that he finished it. He'd never done that before. He met me at the door: you had to go in through a rear entrance. The studio was dark, but he'd placed a lamp just right, and when he turned it on, the light fell full on the *Cordelet.* Can you imagine that? Walking into a dark room and finding the *Cordelet?* I knew immediately it was good: I told him it ranked with Delacroix, Matisse, anything I'd ever seen.

" 'Yes,' he agreed. 'Who would have believed I could create this?' We stood there, both of us, transfixed. And then he went after it. I never even saw where the meat cutter came from. He just had it in his hand, and he was stabbing away like a maniac. The look in his eyes: I knew he'd destroy it, and I couldn't let him do that."

"You could have lost your life," I said.

"He let me take it away from him. The knife . . ."

"I never saw him like that," I said. "It's hard to imagine. I've seen him drunk and sober, up and down. Moods, yes. My God, he was moody. But I never knew him to do anything like that.

"He left it with you. The *Cordelet.*"

"He said he never wanted to hear of it again. I sold it to a collector a few months later and sent him the money. He was on Rimway by then. Later, the collector got five or six times as much for it from an art museum on Rimway. The Apollonian."

3.

At night, the wandering ramps and walkways of Pellinor glitter beneath Fishbowl's spectacular ring system. Its people stroll among softly illuminated parks and malls, which range over the downtown area at, or above, sea level. The trees are healthy here, providing shelter for colorful and noisy avians, most of which are pittacines, imported from Earth and Mogambo. Fishbowl, of course, has no native birds; only the drifting gasbag quill populate her skies.

Pellinor was still a quiet, remote outpost in those days. There were, as yet, few tourists to watch the play of lights against the vertical sea. The Belarian excavations had been abandoned years before, but Survey had retained its foothold on Fishbowl, converting the old support facility into an administrative headquarters.

I can recall sitting on a bench that evening, after my conversation with Stiles. I was on the outer perimeter of the walkways, near the beaches. (They lower it somewhat at night to create a high-tide effect.) On the inland side of the ramp, occasional couples strolled through Survey's geometrical grounds. Above, on the top level, a late party was spilling out of a club.

I had, of course, never been so far from home. Delta Draconis was bright and gold in the north, just visible above the lip of the seawall. And directly overhead, in the wake of the moon, lay Belarius, cool and green and hostile. Home of the *other* civilization: the only nonhuman culture encountered during the long expansion from Earth.

Also to the north, but less than a kilometer away, I could see the cluster of squat buildings that housed Durell's old studio. I walked slowly in that direction, waiting for the lights to dim and the last stragglers to start home. If there were police about, they were not visible. Crime barely existed on Fishbowl. An incident in which several adolescents had stolen a skimmer and crashed at sea, requiring a full-scale rescue, was, ten days later, still a cause of shock and despair.

The smell of the sea was strong. Beyond the beach, it boomed and thundered with soothing effect against the Gantner light screens. I think I knew then that, eventually, the tourists would come, that the wealthy homes out along the ridge would expand, and that Pellinor would lose her innocence. As things turned out, it happened more quickly than I could have expected. But that's another story. The only thing that mattered now, as I got up from my bench and sauntered off to do some burgling, was that, on Fishbowl, locks were simple, and witnesses few.

There had been a skylight. Though he'd never drawn it, its effects were visible in several of his sketches, in the curious double shadow of the latticework, and occasionally of people or pieces of furniture, cast by the twin suns. I reached a strategic location over the rooftops in the commercial district, and looked down on the street in which I'd stood that morning. The rear entrance to Durell's studio, by which Stiles had entered, no longer existed.

I've never been comfortable with heights. The angle at which the ramp crossed the rooftops left only a small corner on which to descend. The pavement was a long way down, and the wind was gusting sharply off the sea.

I clipped a line to the safety rail and, with some misgivings, climbed over the side. Below, a streetlamp threw a wide pool of light around a truck docked at the depot. Two men sat off to one side, talking loudly.

The wind gave me a bad few minutes, pushing me away from the corner of the building. But I got down all right, and made immediately for the skylight.

Any interior walls that might have existed during Durell's time had been removed. I could see a toilet, a sink, and a shower stall toward the rear. Other plumbing fixtures were scattered about. Cartons had been stacked randomly throughout the space, and a couple of hand trucks were in the middle of the floor.

I dropped my line, and, just before climbing in, wondered why the wedge-faced woman had seemed so frightened. A wave of foreboding swept up from the darkness below, and I debated whether it would not be best after all to go home, to forget Coll as best I could, and to accept whatever share of guilt for his death was mine.

I don't know what I was expecting to see: a few plastic-wrapped canvases, maybe, forgotten in a dusty corner. Or possibly a record of some sort. Something.

A rickety table with one drawer held a computer. The drawer was empty. So I wandered around, looking at floors and walls, and eventually staring disconsolately out of the arched front windows at the depot dock across the street. The two men were gone.

I'm not sure what drew my attention to the walls. At the front, where Durell's working studio had been, they were covered with several sheets of bright cheap pastel mosaics. The design was not unattractive, but I knew that Durell could not have lived with it.

That meant the panels had been put up after he'd left. But it seemed unlikely that there'd been another tenant before the area was converted for storage. Why then had anyone bothered to decorate the walls?

The sheets were thick with dust. I peeled off a long strip of trim, removed the baseboard, and released the magnets. (I heard the whine of a set of gyros, and the truck rose past the windows. Its lights fell across the front windows, and then were gone.) The panel was wedged at the top and on one side. I pried it forward and tried to get the lamp behind it.

Light fell on the outline of an ear. My blood quickened: the lines were the quick, precise strokes of Durell Coll! I put the light down, braced my back against the wall, and broke the panel. It went with a bang.

I snapped off the lamp, and waited to see if I'd attracted anyone's notice. But there were no footsteps in the street or on the stairs. Nevertheless, as my alarm faded, I stood a long time in the dark, savoring the moment.

The sea was loud. It was easy to understand why Durell, working on this world, amid the endless tidal roar, would have found his meanings ultimately in the natural world. To my knowledge, he had never before done a portrait.

I lifted the lamp to get a good look. . . .

If Durell Coll's reputation was built on gloomy perceptions of a hostile universe, the man himself, at least during his early years on Rimway, had always enjoyed a good party. He was usually surrounded by women, and loved to spend the long winter evenings (we lived high in the northern hemisphere) talking and drinking with old friends.

He laughed easily; and nothing amused him more than suggestions by people who should have known better that his work needed cheering up. More vitality, they used to say. More life.

It was only toward the end that the shadows that had been lengthening from his art began, finally, to darken his features. And a Durell Coll that I did not know appeared, a man who took solitary strolls through snow-filled streets, who endured intense nightmares of which he would not speak, and who ultimately withdrew into a world not unlike that of the *Cordelet.*

It was the early Durell that I preferred to remember, and whom I'd hoped to find in the old studio.

What I found instead was something dredged out of the soul of a madman: a face barely human, rendered in Durell's painfully realistic fashion. It was of a man in middle age, with a full beard and commanding features. But his terror-ridden eyes gaped out of deep black sockets. The mouth was twisted into a frightful snarl, and flecks of saliva flew from the beard.

I stumbled backward and fell over a hand truck. The light went out again, and this time I was not at all anxious to put it back on. Instead, I simply lay in the dark, listening to the sound of my own breathing, feeling the palpable presence of the thing on the wall, trying to understand how a young Durell Coll, *my* Durell, could have created the monstrosity.

There was no doubt it was *his* work. Despite the lurid nature of the subject, tone and line were clearly his.

I'd bruised an elbow, and gradually the pain intruded itself. I rubbed it, grateful for the distraction.

The bearded man was a stranger. I wondered whether he'd actually existed, or whether Coll unaided had conceived and executed the tortured image.

In a sense, I supposed I had what I'd come for: an unknown work by Durell, a previously unsuspected creation. It would be worth a lot of money.

But not to me.

The image appeared, at first, to be badly faded, until I realized that someone had painted over it. (And then, not satisfied, had covered the result with panels.) But over the years, the paint had faded, and only the image remained.

And the other panels: What lay under them? I played my light across the swirl of spring colors, and my heart sank.

The sensible thing to have done at that point would have been to leave. God knows I wanted to get out of there, and off Fishbowl, and to put behind me, somehow, the last four years of my life.

I removed a second panel. There was enough light from outside to see that there was another figure, although I could make out no details. This one came off easily, and I laid it on the floor before turning my attention to the wall. I was ready this time. Nevertheless, I did not look directly into its eyes.

It was the same hideous figure.

A third, smaller, rendering of the subject was partly covered by the next panel.

I was slow to realize that the three images, however, were not identical. The angle of the profile changed from one to another, the light in the eyes was subtly different in each, the beard . . . I took them all down, ten or eleven panels: the same face appeared again and again, its grotesque expression, each time, varied in some way. As though the artist were experimenting.

My Durell. The gentlest, most sensitive human being I had known.

I replaced the panels, thinking the whole time that, if I could, I would gladly have razed the walls, or destroyed the building. No wonder the proprietor of the crockery shop had been frightened of me.

4.

Fishbowl's chess club meets in a glass-lined conference room on the second level of a flattened pyramid, located on Survey's grounds, adjacent the main administration building, and known simply as the Annex. On the night I visited it, there were about twelve games in progress, and one spectator, a laser-eyed elderly woman, who immediately challenged me to play.

I declined politely, whispering that I did not understand the game (an explanation which prompted a brief look of sympathy), and inquired whether she'd ever heard of Durell. She hadn't, and I settled in to watch for an opportunity to ask someone else. The only sounds in the room were the occasional scraping of chairs against the floor, and the chimes of the chess clocks.

It was difficult to predict when a game was going to end. Players had a tendency to resign merely by stopping the clock. Then, within moments, they'd reset the pieces and begun again. Not that it mattered: when I attempted to whisper questions, people shook their heads in irritation, and looked pointedly around at games-in-progress.

I retired from the field of combat, and settled for intercepting players on their way to the washroom. Two or three remembered Durell, but only as someone who came occasionally to the club. ("Liked to play the Dragon Variation of the Sirian, but he was far to cautious.")

Toward the end of the evening, I approached Jon Hollander, who was one of the club's officers. His face was ruddy and undisciplined, his jaw slack, and his eyes tired. Someone told me later that chess was the consuming passion of his life, and that he wasn't very good at it. "I don't recall him, Tiel, but we've had a lot of members over the years. What precisely did you want to know?" He looked at me the way men do when they've been a long time without a woman.

I had no idea. "I suppose I just wanted to talk with someone who'd known him," I said.

"And you couldn't find anybody?"

"Not really."

He smiled for no particular reason. "Maybe we can find something in the archives."

We left the clubroom, and turned into a long carpeted corridor that curved and rose until we'd ascended approximately a level. He led the way into an office, and sat down at a terminal. "There may not be anything," he said, "but we can try."

I nodded, he brought up the screen, and punched in Durell's name. Dates and numbers appeared. "He was a member for almost two years." He grinned. "He had some problems paying his dues."

"What else do you have?"

"Address and code number. You want those?"

"No."

Hollander bent over the screen. "How about one of his games? We have three on record."

"No, I don't think so."

"Looks like he lost them all anyhow."

"You don't have a picture of him, do you?"

Hollander pushed a pad, and an index appeared. "No," he said, running his eye down the names. "We have several group photos from the period when he was a member, but he doesn't seem to be in any of them." The index faded, to be replaced by several people in parkas, standing outside the Annex during a snowstorm. "The Second Winter Open. Coll played in that tournament, but I guess he wasn't around when they took the picture." Another group appeared, still cold weather, but the snow was gone. "This was our first Masters', the same year. He wasn't eligible for that one."

He changed it again, for an indoor shot. But something had struck me about the Winter Open, and I didn't know what. "Go back to the first one, Jon," I said.

The snow scene reappeared. Three women were seated on a bench, in front of four men. "That's me, on the left," said Hollander.

"Who's that beside you?"

He squinted. "Looks like Ux." The man was bigger than Hollander, but shorter than either of the other two. Although his hood was tied tightly down against the obvious chill of the day, he wore a wide smile. Hollander brought his image up. "Yes," he said. "It's Reuben Uxbridge. Did you know him?"

I knew him: his was the face on the wall. "Who is he?"

Hollander's features softened. "He was a charter member. One of the strongest players we've ever had. He specialized in the end game. Once he got the queens off the board—"

"Where is he now?"

"Ux died quite a few years ago, Tiel."

Down the long corridor, I could hear voices as the playing room emptied out. "What happened to him? He looks reasonably young."

Hollander cupped his chin in his palms. "He drowned. I guess it was only a year or so after the picture was taken." His eyes grew thoughtful. "Queer business. He walked out onto a beach near his home one day in midsummer. A couple of families were there on an outing. And he went past them without saying a word and simply walked into the sea."

He turned slowly in my direction, but his eyes were focused far off someplace. "Why?" I asked.

He shrugged. "He'd changed since he came back from Belarius. He was here for about two years before they went to Belarius. When they came back, less than a year later, he was changed. I don't know why."

"Wasn't that the second attempt?" I asked.

"Yes," he said. "I guess both expeditions more or less blew up. The official word put out was that there were hostile conditions. Ux never talked about it and, to my knowledge, no one ever pressed him with questions. But something happened to him. At one point, there was talk that he'd brought something back."

"How did he change?"

"I don't know, exactly. For one thing, his game improved. No, don't look at me like that: I mean really improved. He threw himself into his chess. Played like a man possessed. He opened up, and abandoned his old precise positional play for a ferocious combinative style. Listen, Tiel, chess players can change their approach to the game, but I never saw anything like what happened to Ux. It was like he was a different person." He rose slowly and shut down the computer. "Furthermore, during that latter stage, he was the strongest player we had.

"That wasn't the only thing. He became withdrawn, didn't talk much to anyone. That kind of condition has to become pretty severe before you notice it in a chess club."

We retraced our steps to the playing room. There were still a few games going. "Did he have a family? Anyone I might talk to?"

"No," said Hollander. "None that I know of. But I can give you a list of people who knew him. Everyone liked him."

"Who was with him on Belarius?"

He shook his head. "Nobody here. They still have some people over at Survey who made the second flight. They'll remember him."

"You mean there are no employees in Survey's chess club?"

"They just lend us the space, Tiel."

"Is it a coincidence," I asked, "that Uxbridge's name is the same as the bay's? The one at the far end of the island?"

"That's the only bay we got. No: it's no coincidence. He lived out there. At the Point."

"Jon," I said, "I was there yesterday, and I didn't see any house. Not in the area of the bay, anyhow."

"You wouldn't," he said. "It's under the bay now. Shortly

after Ux died, somebody took a laser to the projector on the Point, and let the sea in. Pity: it was a fine house."

I could feel my scalp beginning to prickle. "Jon, that sounds as if you've been inside it."

"A few times," he said. "He used to invite me, or Arkady, or one of the others out occasionally to play a few games." His eyes closed, and a rueful smile appeared. "He had a kind of trophy room at the back of the house, filled with plaques and artifacts and whatnot. And two leather chairs he'd brought with him from Rimway. Tiel, they were probably the only leather chairs on Fishbowl! Those were fine evenings. And good chess."

"Jon, was this before he went to Belarius?"

"Oh yes." He nodded. "I don't think anybody ever went out there after he came back. The invitations stopped. At least mine did. Although, now that I think of it, he came to my place now and then. He just didn't reciprocate any more." He'd turned away and was looking out through the glass. Fishbowl's rings were visible over the Admin Building.

"The destruction of the seawall," he continued, "created some commotion, because people thought maybe we had a loony running around who was planning to sink the island. For a while they posted guards at all the projector stations, but nothing more ever happened, and I guess they finally decided it was just some kids. Now, the projectors are pretty well shielded."

"They never made repairs?"

He looked at me apologetically. "Draining it again and reestablishing the screen would have been expensive, so we never bothered. No one ever stepped forward to take a proprietary interest. There've been proposals to go in and reclaim the land, but there's really no reason to. So we named the bay after him instead."

I showed him the holo of the *Cordelet.* "Is this what we're talking about?"

"Yes," he said. "That's it. The house is down there somewhere. Right about in the middle, I'd think."

I wondered if it had ever occurred to anyone that some-body had specifically wanted to destroy Uxbridge's home.

5.

In the morning, I rented a skimmer. But, instead of turn-ing south and running down the coastline, I procrastinated, hovering aimlessly over Pellinor for an hour, and then drift-ing out to sea. I kept low, just above the waves, until my clothes were drenched with spray. Behind me, the land had vanished into a hole in the ocean, bracketed by the cluster of brown hills to the south, and the upper levels of Pellinor's wide ramps.

I settled into the water. Gideon was sliding behind lumpy columns of cumulus. The white rim of Heli was just pushing out of the sea, and the color of the sky was changing minute by minute.

I'm not sure how long I sat out there, listening to the water lap against the sideboards, thinking about the madness in the eyes on the walls, and the strange behavior of Reuben Uxbridge. If Hollander was correct, Uxbridge had under-gone a basic personality change. There was an eerie resem-blance to Durell.

I was no longer sure I wanted to know the truth, but I did not wish to be driven at some future date to return to Fish-bowl because I couldn't sleep well. What had begun as an innocent nostalgic excursion had become something radi-cally different.

I buckled myself in, left the shields down so I could feel the rush of air, and started back. Only the drifting quill, their fibrilla dangling into the waves, broke the monotony of sea and sky. An ocean with a single shore gets little traffic.

Just off the Point, a school of large marine animals were sunning themselves. There must have been a hundred or more, huge creatures, of the stature of our behemoth, or perhaps the sperm whale of Earth's oceans. They moved slowly, and their great dark eyes rolled curiously skyward to watch me pass. The articulation of fin and jaw was not so fine or detailed as I was accustomed to, but Fishbowl is a young world.

Abruptly, the sea fell away, and I was over the rills and valleys of the island. Then they too gave way, though not with the same breathtaking suddenness, to the burnished surface of Uxbridge Bay.

The mood of my first visit was gone: the sense of a place out of time, of a world with psychic links to an earlier age, had evaporated. And in its stead, despite the bright morning suns, I sensed only madness and despair.

I rose high over the crystal waters, slowed to a few klicks, and locked in the pilot. Out near the Point, behind the arc of hills that constrained the bay, lay a series of sandy beaches. I wondered which had been the one from which the unfortunate Uxbridge had strolled to his death.

The bay was almost perfectly circular. This was a feature not apparent in the *Cordelet,* where the harbor mouth appears quite distant, and the far shore rather near, suggesting a more elongated shape. Close in, the bottom was littered with rocks. But it was relatively clear, despite rippling shadows cast by currents, and clumps of undulating sea anima. Not far from the place where I'd stood my first day surveying the scene lay a line of rocks. Paralleling the coastline for a considerable distance, they were either a collapsed breakwater or the remains of a wall.

I dropped lower and flew in wide circles that took me well out to sea on each pass. There was no sign of a house, and I had about decided that either the story was fabricated or that everything had been destroyed. I was riding listlessly over the mouth of the bay when I saw the shadow in the water.

I lobbed a cone buoy over the side, came around, and, too absorbed perhaps to pay attention to what I was doing, cut power before I was fully down. The skimmer chopped heavily into the water, bounced, jabbed its nose below the surface, and threatened briefly to turn over.

I blamed it on the lighter gravity, took a quick look around for damage (there was none), and got out a deep-sided glass dish I'd brought along for submarine viewing. I was right over the house, and it looked intact. That struck me as being exceedingly unlikely, until I noticed a small ridge cutting diagonally down from the shoreline and across the bottom of the basin. Driven into it, and now broken off, were a pair of stems of the type that provided nominal support for a Gantner light system.

That meant Uxbridge's house had been entirely, or at least partly, above the flood. But the water had got at the projector and shorted it out. The increased weight had snapped the stems, and the place had gone to the bottom.

It was a three-level structure, apparently made of stone rather than the standardized materials generally in use on Fishbowl. The external appurtenances, stylized cupolas, belvederes, porticoes, and so on, that characterize most of the wealthy homes on Fishbowl (and on Rimway, for that matter) were particularly in evidence here. Add small, round windows, and the illusion of an exotic sea beast lying quietly in the sand was complete.

But the windows were dark, and only fish swam through its abandoned rooms.

It had no tower.

I'd brought a breather with me, and I knew that the next rational step was to use it. But the house was far down, and the suspicion of what I might find prevented my unpacking the unit. Instead, I sat rocking gently on the skimmer, feeling like a damned fool.

After a while I started the engine and rolled angrily into the bright clear sky.

6.

When Jon Hollander looks through the windows from the office in which the Pellinor Chess Club keeps its records, he can see a broad oval pool. Directly beyond the pool crouches a heavy, triple-tiered oblate building utterly out of place among the crystal structures of the Survey complex. This is the Belarian Field Museum. It is, according to a plaque mounted at the front entrance, an accurate representation of architectural styles to be found at Ysdril West, one of the major excavation sites in that world's southern hemisphere.

One recognizes immediately that it is the work of a primitive people. Constructed of quartz, the Field Museum is encircled by a pavilion whose roof rests on a series of square-cut columns. According to the plaque, the roof is 0.3 meters higher than it would have been on the original, to accommodate its human visitors. Entryways and overheads have been proportionately raised. The upper tiers are progressively recessed, creating an effect somewhat like that of a ziggurat.

The quartz blocks are rough-hewn and joined with cement. Nightmare creatures with bared fangs and talons guard the entrances, and hieroglyphs have been stenciled into the living rock, marking each of the four principal directions. The inscriptions are delicate, sylphlike engravings, utterly out of character with the ponderous stone blocks and doors.

I'd paused on the west portico to examine one, tracing the lean characters with my fingers. A plate translated: "In the hour of need, I am with you."

The windows were small, recessed, and barred. The descriptive material on the plaque announced that the structure was a place of worship, but it felt like a fortress.

I wasn't entirely ignorant about the Belarians. They'd been small creatures, by human standards, seldom surpassing a meter in height. Artists' renderings of their appearance were disquieting, however: pale, bloated, gas-filled bodies, not unlike the quill, which possess neither distinctive limbs nor organs, nor even separate body parts.

They never achieved a technological culture, and the last of them went to their reward a million years ago. I'd never really thought about it before, but standing in the shadow of that gloomy pile, I wondered how creatures without external limbs had constructed a written language. Or, for that matter, juggled building supplies.

I walked in under a blunt arch. The ground floor of the interior was crowded with display cases, statuary, tools, and assorted other artifacts. An attendant in Survey's light and dark green uniform stood beside a stone altar, behind which several viewing booths had been installed. To my right, a ramp ascended to the upper levels.

I was surprised to discover an abundance of natural light emanating from a circular courtyard. The overall effect was, I suppose, like that of any museum: a place in which one felt bored, but pretended to be awed, by the collected junk of dead persons who had lived in some quaint manner.

Besides myself, there was only one visitor, a brittle, elderly man who was sketching an inscription from a hexagonal stone mounted over a display board. I walked among the artifacts, little figures carved from black rock set in gleaming cases with neat white cards identifying their probable age and use.

There were scrapers and cutters and rakeheads and spearpoints. Obviously, the Belarians were more substantial than they looked. There were figures of animals and dwellings, and fantastic creatures that might have been real or mythical. One case contained several hundred tablets, all stamped with rows of ideographs. A plate placed them quite early in Belarian history. They had not yet been translated, although it was from similar, though somewhat later, materials that the Book of Life, with its immortal accounts of Cordelet and the pillars of the world, had been derived.

"They had paper," said a voice behind me. "It's ironic that only the earliest written materials have survived. Only the tablets." It was the old man. He was about my size, clean-shaven except for a neatly trimmed white mustache. (That was not, then, the style on Fishbowl, and marked him as a hopeless relic.) "Even the inscriptions on their buildings are from early religious or ethical texts. The books are all gone."

"I'm Tiel Chadwick," I said, offering my hand.

He took it in a firm grasp. "M'Kay Alexander. You may call me Alex."

I described myself as an art student from Rimway, and we

talked for a while about Belarian art. Other than architecture, little remained.

"How did they produce anything?" I asked. "I mean, they had no hands."

"They had a highly flexible sheath," he replied. "Pseudopodal extensions. If you look closely, you can see them on some of the artifacts. Here . . ." He pointed to a pair of figures in an adjoining case. They did indeed seem to have limbs. Though they emerged from disconcerting locations: from abdominal and head areas, if you attempted to visualize the creature as a human being under a sheet.

Okay: that seemed reasonable enough. But what about the buildings? You can't move a boulder with a pseudopod. "They must have had heavy equipment of some kind."

"Not that we could find, Chadwick. No: it was often difficult to sort things out among them, there was so little left. But I don't think they ever had the sort of machines that would be required to haul these blocks around."

"How do you know?"

"Their psychology. They were simply not a technological people. Did you know their culture was twenty thousand years old when they died off? And they never got past a medieval stage."

"What happened to them?"

"One theory is that the competition was too severe. Or that they couldn't unite politically. Or technological stagnation. Who knows?" He was turning the pages of his sketch pad, holding it so I could see. It was filled with renderings of the objects in the cases, or the altar, and of the Field Museum itself. "It's a puzzle, how they moved these rocks around. It's one of the things Survey was trying to find out when they were driven off."

I blinked at the old man: I hadn't heard it put in quite those terms before. "What drove them off?"

Alexander placed his fingertips against the altar, as though he could read something in the cold stone. "I'd love to know," he said.

"Wasn't it ever made public?" I asked.

"In a way, Tiel. They released a fairly detailed description of conditions on Belarius after the second expedition. It's an old world: there's been a lot of time for evolution. So the carnivores are very efficient. They have a lot of teeth, and they move very quickly, and some of them fly, and most of them are hard to see coming." I'd seen pictures of a few. The one that stuck in my mind was a kind of jet-propelled airborne shark. "And they are reasonably intelligent. Which, by the way, has been a factor in keeping their numbers down, so that they don't eliminate the food supply."

"How do you mean?" We were standing idly among the displays, near a diorama of the Ysdril West excavation.

"They made war on one another. The species did."

"Why?"

"For the same reason animals fight on Rimway. Hunting rights. Except that on Belarius, it was organized warfare. The species there seem to have more than their share of intelligence and administrative capacity. In any case, I can't imagine why a well-armed force—and, at least in the case of the second expedition, forewarned as well—couldn't hold their own against local predators."

"Alex, you seem to know quite a lot about Belarius. Have you worked for Survey?"

He looked around for a place to sit, and found a stone bench. "I'm in the food business," he said. "Or was. I'm retired now."

I couldn't suppress a smile. "How does somebody in the food business come to be involved in all this?" I waved an arm around.

"We have a little group on Rimway," he said. "Mostly people like me, who are just interested in the Belarian story." He leaned forward, his voice intent. "Listen, Tiel, Survey's not telling the truth about what happened on Belarius. Moreover, it's been years now since they officially announced that they would not go back there. But look over there!" He pointed through the front entrances at the pool, and at the cluster of Survey buildings beyond. They were silver and green in the late afternoon light. "Why have they stayed on Fishbowl? God knows it's not near anything. There's nothing out here."

I shrugged.

"Because," he said, "they're going back! Tiel, there is no possibility that, after looking all this time, they're going to walk off and leave what they've found."

The attendant stared curiously over at us.

The diorama was mostly sand: a collection of partly uncovered blocks and columns, earth-moving machines, temporary shelters, and people. A lander stood on the edge of the display. No single indigenous structure was intact. "Alex," I said, "I take it you've not been to Belarius?"

"No," he said, with regret. "When we heard about the second mission, we pooled our money, and offered Survey a substantial sum to allow passage to one of our members. If they'd gone along with it, we were going to cut cards to decide the winner."

"What did they say?"

"Too dangerous. They couldn't take the responsibility." His eyes narrowed. "I can't quarrel with that. They lost almost half the landing team on the first effort. The second try wasn't much better." He stared at Ysdril West. "But I would have liked to go."

I'd been wondering whether Durell might have made the trip, but I dismissed the possibility. "Alex," I said, "there were several excavation sites on Belarius. This place is pretty well dead. Are they all like this?"

"You mean in ruins? Oh yes. This is the best preserved."

"Is there a tower anywhere?"

"Intact?"

I hesitated over that one. "Not necessarily. Anything sticking up out of the rubble that one could describe as a tower."

He thought about it. "No," he said finally. "I don't think so. If there is, they're keeping it quiet."

"Do you know anything about Reuben Uxbridge?"

"He was an expert on ideographic structure." He glanced at his watch, and then shrugged. "Damned thing's no good here anyhow. But I have to be going." He stood up. "Uxbridge worked for Casmir Moss. I don't think he did anything important."

"Was he ever involved in any sort of unusual incident?"

"Tiel, I would say they were all involved in unusual incidents of one kind or another. I just don't know. If you want to talk to someone about Uxbridge, see Moss."

"Where would I find him?"

"He's here somewhere. He's one of the reasons I'm sure they're going back. Moss would have more important things to do than hang around Fishbowl if something weren't about to happen."

Two middle-aged women and a boy came in. The boy made immediately for the diorama. "Alex," I asked, "are you here alone?"

"Yes," he said. "Three of us were supposed to make the trip, but things came up. You know how it is."

"How about dinner?" I said. "My treat."

7.

That night, I punched up everything the Library had on the two missions. The official stuff wasn't very informative, and the dozen or so books written on the subject were neither consistent with each other nor helpful. Eggleston's *Bureaucrats in the Field* mercilessly flayed security procedures that "couldn't hold off a few wild animals with modern weapons." Adrian Hunt, in *Survey and Belarius: A Study in the Exercise of Power,* maintained that the political appointees who control Survey's funding wished to put an end to the program because it cost too much, and the feudal civilization that had developed on Belarius could in no conceivable way make a contribution to Confederate technology. Other volumes hinted darkly at a demonic presence on Belarius. (Or under it, I suppose.)

There was no mention of Uxbridge anywhere, but Eggleston excoriated Moss as an incompetent paper-shuffler who'd been more concerned with arcane languages than with the practical hazards faced by his teams. (Moss's division of philologists and archaeologists had taken the heaviest losses, and he was charged with providing inadequate security training for himself and his subordinates.)

Like Uxbridge, Moss was a philologist, though of somewhat more advanced reputation. He'd won most of the major awards, declined at least two university presidencies, and written *The Dawn of Language*, the definitive study of proto-Sumerian ideography. Eggleston remarked that, for Moss, the Belarian discovery was a kind of fresh virgin after the long line of ancients so thoroughly worked over by everybody else.

But this had apparently been a virgin with a bite.

The evening after my conversation with M'Kay Alexander, I contrived to be at Arnholf's, a small restaurant overlooking a shopping quadrangle, when Moss came in for his evening meal. He was a man of quite ordinary appearance, with dull blue eyes, and defensive lines drawn about his mouth. It would have been no surprise to learn that he made his living from dead languages.

I maneuvered into a table adjacent his, ordered some seafood (what else?), and awaited an opportunity. Moss took some papers from a case, spread them in front of him, and sank immediately into a reverie.

Along about the time the wine came, his and mine, he looked up to catch me quizzically staring at him. That was my cue. "Pardon me," I said, rising and advancing, "but aren't you Casmir Moss?"

"I am," he said, apparently not entirely displeased at being recognized.

"I'm Tiel Chadwick," I said. "I've read your book." That was a wild gamble. What I meant to say, of course, was that I'd read *of* it.

He smiled back uncertainly, inviting me to say something else. I did. I told him that it had sparked my interest in ancient civilizations, and that I thought he'd made difficult concepts quite lucid.

Within a few minutes, we were drinking from the same

carafe. He loved to talk about Babylonian politics, and I encouraged him, asked a few safe questions and, later in the evening, found myself strolling with him along the beachfront. Abruptly, he turned and faced me. "Who are you, really?"

The question caught me by surprise. "A friend of Ux's," I said.

He was silent for a time. The moon drifted low on the ocean, limning the incoming waves with silver. Eventually, gripping the safety rail, he told me he was sorry.

We walked out past the Oceanographic Institute, saying little and, at my suggestion, stopped at a little bar on the edge of a park. "Reuben Uxbridge," he said, as we entered, "was one of the most difficult people I've ever worked with. He didn't like to take directions, thought anyone disputing his views was misinformed, and generally behaved abrasively to everyone. But my God, I would give a lot to have him with us tonight."

That didn't sound much like the Uxbridge the chess players knew. Of course, the circumstances were different. I'd intended to wait until we'd gone through two or three rounds. But the moment had clearly arrived. We ordered a couple of drinks and retired with them to a booth. He sipped his, studying the liquid in the wavering light of a candle. "Casmir," I said, "What happened in the tower room?"

His eyes widened perceptibly. "I did not think he would tell anyone. How much do you know?"

"Very little."

"I assume you are aware of conditions on Belarius?"

"I know they're difficult."

"I would say violent." He smiled, as at some private joke. "But the prize was well worth the risk. Did Ux tell you why we were so interested in Ysdril West? No? Then let me: it is not one city, but seven: built over tens of thousands of years on the same site. Like Troy on the Dardanelles. It was a strategic location. No matter how often the city died, later generations returned and built a new one. Ysdril West was such a place: in ancient times, it stood on a narrow neck of land dividing two continents. But climatic changes pushed the oceans back, the land dropped and dried out, and the place was buried in a desert.

"We've been able to follow the development of their languages over much of the history of the culture. Let me tell you what that means, Tiel: it means that we can begin, finally, to separate those perceptions that are induced by environment, including one's own physical wrapping, from those that are of the essence of a thinking species."

I could see that he was warming to his subject, so I tried to steer him back. "The tower, Doctor. Where was the tower?"

"On the eastern edge of the city. It was probably a beacon of some sort at one time, to warn off vessels approaching too close to the coast. We couldn't be sure because the top sections were gone. Obviously the place had been looted in later days by vandals, but the bastards had at least had the good sense to shut the doors behind them."

I understood why I'd found no tower in the diorama. It extended down, rather than up. "Dr. Moss, did you know Durell Coll?"

He looked puzzled. "No," he said. "Should I?"

"No: I'm sorry. Please go on."

"The tower was a Level III structure, which is to say it was part of the third most recent city. But it was curious because some of the inscriptions we found, not on the walls themselves, but in artifacts found inside, were of a later period. That suggested that the Belarians themselves maintained the place as a monument of some sort. They had a historical sense, Tiel! You will understand we were anxious to get into the lower levels.

"The upper compartments were filled with sand and, in some places, blocked by collapsed walls. And we were worried we might destroy something. So the work was slow. To make things more difficult, Belarius has a wide variety of exotic predators, and they are hard to discourage. We must have killed hundreds of one kind and another, but there were limits to what we could do. Sometimes people disappeared. Or were devoured in full view of a work crew. Or were carried off. Gradually, we got better, but we discovered we had to devote more and more of our people to the defenses.

"We'd originally assumed that it would be necessary to excavate the entire structure, but about a quarter of the way down, the quantity of sand in succeeding compartments began to decline, until it had nearly ended altogether. Then it became merely a matter of opening heavy doors.

"There were inscriptions on the walls, mostly of a religious nature. These were quite sophisticated, by the way." He began an analysis of Belarian syntax. This time I let him go, and tried to show some enthusiasm. Another round of drinks came. And I began to suspect he didn't want to continue his story.

"Was Ux directing the excavation?" I asked.

"Oh no," he said. "We had an archaeologist to do that, the detail work. Chellic Oberrif. We brought her in especially for the tower operation. She'd done something similar at the excavations of the early settlements on Mogambo. She was good."

I thought his eyes misted a little. "There was a place at the hundred and thirty meter level, about two thirds of the way down, though we didn't know it then, of course, that blocked us for days. Whole chambers and connecting corridors had collapsed. The danger was that an attempt to cut through might bring down the entire structure. God knows it was shaky enough. But she looped a tunnel around the obstruction, and reentered further down.

"When we did manage later to excavate those sections, we found weapons and remains. A battle of some sort had been fought in there, and one side or the other had tripped a mechanism that buried the contending parties. We have no idea what the argument was about.

"What was important, however, was that the vandals and robbers of later periods had been unable to penetrate below the battle site. In the lower compartments, we found furniture, religious regalia, the stuff of daily life. It was, of course, incredibly old, and a lot of it was dust. But it was there.

"And at the base of the tower, we found a single wide oval room, with an altar raised in its center. A big one, maybe three times the size of the one in the Field Museum. We filed down into the chamber from a position immediately behind the altar. Several smaller compartments opened off on the sides. Directly in front, we were looking through an arch into a tunnel. Chellic hurried immediately around to it, barely glancing at anything else. 'We're down at least one level,' she said.

"We were at the end of a long workday. I proposed that we continue in the morning, but Uxbridge wouldn't have it. We sent the work crew back up, though Chellic, of course, insisted on coming with us.

"She was even more obsessed with the possibilities of the place than Ux. She'd made it a point to acquaint herself with the various ideographic systems that we'd solved, and had become a valuable contributor to our ongoing analysis. She was, in addition, a good shot. On one occasion, I watched her coolly stand her ground during a general assault and kill four or five pickeyes."

"Pickeyes?"

"They're birds, very small, and very fast. The name is deserved. Anyhow, we started in. We were using oxygen. Our radio contact on the surface advised us to return. Bendimeyer, who was the security chief, didn't like unscheduled activities. I wish to hell we'd obliged him.

"But we were all intoxicated by then. My God, I can still remember the exhilaration of that walk out into the buried city. Until then, all we had of anything below Level II was the satellite scans.

"The tunnels were low, and we couldn't stand up straight. It was hard on the back. Even on me, so you can imagine how Ux felt.

"I remember Chellic saying how there was enough down there for a lifetime. We saw murals, metalwork, tools, even petrified gardens. We found a library in one room. But the books were dust.

"It was raining on the surface. We were looking at a scullery when Bendimeyer got on the radio. We knew immediately we had a problem because he should have been asleep by then. 'Moss,' he said, 'we got a critter in the tower. It's started down, so you may hear from it.' I asked what it was. 'We don't know,' he said. 'Nobody got a very good look. It's bipedal, we think. Rodley says it's about Ux's size. Big.'

"We'd been on Belarius long enough to know that nothing that travels alone is harmless. But we were armed, and we hadn't found anything yet that a bolt wouldn't stop. The thing that concerned me was that we couldn't see very far down there.

"I asked Bendimeyer to inform me if the critter emerged again. He said they were sending a team after it, and I asked him not to. 'It'll only drive it in on top of us. Anyway, I don't want nervous guys with weapons in front of me. We're starting back.'

"Chellic suggested we might be better off to wait it out. 'The damned thing could never find us in this labyrinth,' she said. But Ux argued that we didn't know what kind of senses it might have, and that we were safer if we could make the tower room. I asked him why. 'Because there are too many places here where several corridors converge. We can't watch everything. If we can get back to the tower before it gets all the way down, we only have to worry about what's ahead of us.'

"Chellic concurred, and we got moving. Nobody was much interested now in the galleries and public rooms through which we passed. I'd been making notes as we proceeded, to avoid our getting lost. But we managed to take a couple of wrong turns anyhow, and lost time backtracking.

"After a while, Chellic suggested that, since we had no idea of the creature's capabilities, we should assume that it had already got into the lower levels, and that it might come from any direction. 'The thing,' she added, looking meaningfully past Ux's shoulder, 'could even be behind us.'

"Imagination raises hell under those circumstances. If you listen hard enough, you always hear something. I could make out claws scraping on stone, breathing in the walls, you name it. I drew my laser, though walking with a lamp in one hand and a weapon in the other was distinctly inconvenient. But it felt reassuring.

"Ux fell over a hole at one point and twisted his knee. He was looking behind him at the time, and went down hard. The weapon discharged, and drilled a neat round hole through the wall. We had to help him along after that, but nobody wanted to stop, so we kept moving. There wasn't much talk.

"I checked back periodically with Bendimeyer. They were sitting at the top of the excavation with a small arsenal, but they'd seen nothing come out." Moss took a deep breath. Sweat had begun to drip down his neck and into his shirt. The narrative was taking on a life of its own: he needed no further encouragement from me.

"The places we were most worried about, of course, were the compartments with a profusion of entrances and exits. We hurried through them as quickly as we could, expecting every moment the wild attack that we knew was inevitable.

"Ux held up pretty well, and Chellic had turned into some kind of goddam jungle animal herself. I wasn't very happy about the situation, but I felt good about the people I was with.

"We stopped occasionally to check our bearings, and rest our backs. It was during one of these halts, as we drew close to the the base of the tower, that I had a sudden sensation of terrible hunger. The lights dimmed, and I glanced at Chellic beside me, her head bent between her knees, her neck exposed under the hairline." Moss sat stiffly erect. He put his empty glass carefully on the table, holding his fingers around its rim. His eyes swiveled round, and locked with mine. "I thought how good it would be to bury my teeth in her."

I sat in shocked silence. His breath whistled through clenched teeth. "The sensation, the *urge*, lasted only an instant. But it left me weak and terrified.

"When we started out again, Chellic had to stop to help me. And I was afraid to let her touch me. Ux asked whether I was all right. I told him I was, and increased my oxygen. But

Chellic knew something had happened, and she made no effort to move on until I signaled I was ready to go.

"We came finally into the tower room, I was relieved to see the altar, and the wide, curving wall: it meant no more multiple entrances to be watched. Ux threw his lamplight around the chamber to be sure it was empty, and examined the series of adjoining compartments. Chellic climbed the ramp behind the altar and looked into the tunnel ahead, while I kept a nervous eye on the way we'd come. 'We should be all right now,' Chellic said, her features softening in the lamplight. Even with a pickax in her belt, she was a lovely woman."

Moss's hands gripped the arms of his chair. "There was really no other way to proceed," he said, his voice hardly a whisper. "No finding of guilt ever came out of it. Even now, knowing what I know, I cannot see what we might have done differently. But, my God, there must have been a way . . ." His eyes squeezed shut.

"Ux suggested we rest awhile before continuing. He eased himself down against a rock slab, and placed his lamp on top of it, aimed into the passage through which we would leave. The lasers are big-barreled things, not like the modest weapons that Survey teams are routinely equipped with. These were military issue at one time. At short range and high register, nothing that lives could survive even a peripheral hit. Under all that rock, of course, we had to be careful, but you will understand we had no doubts about our weapons.

"I kept mine at hand the whole time. Ux was still limping badly, and it was obvious he was glad to get off the knee. But he seemed more worried about me, and asked several times if I was all right." Moss's face reddened a bit, and he managed a weak smile. "He said nothing along those lines to Chellic.

"Then it happened again: Chellic had walked over near the altar and begun to move through a series of stretching exercises. While I watched her, the chamber began to darken. I could sense her long limbs beneath the coveralls, see the suggestion of breast and shoulder: the blood was warm in her shoulders, and I could taste . . ." Moss's eyes filled with tears. He shook his head savagely, leaped from his seat, and hurried out into the night. I ignored the stares of people around us, dropped some money on the table, and followed.

He was staring up at the vertical sea. Reflections from the city lights played against its surface. "If I had my way," he said bitterly, "we'd kill everything on that world and be done with it. Introduce a bug, attack the food chain, tickle a couple of volcanoes. Whatever it takes. But I'd clear that goddam world once and for all." He jammed his fists into his pockets and looked at me with tears in his eyes. "Did Ux ever tell you any of this?"

"No," I said, trying not to feel guilty. "Maybe that's why he drowned himself."

Moss laughed. It was an ugly sound. "Tiel, I've told this story a hundred times. I've told it to Survey, to analysts, to drunks in bars. I'll live with it forever. Just like Uxbridge did.

"I was with it when it walked into the chamber. I felt the water-cold rock beneath padded feet, and the dusty air sucked down past curving rows of incisors. I looked from Ux to Chellic to myself, delaying the moment of selection even though I knew, knew from the beginning. The lean one, Chellic, had been on its feet and turned to face me. The light from the lamps had acquired an amber tint. I, we, knew our danger. The three—things—were terribly slow, but all had burners.

"It hesitated. We wanted Chellic, and we advanced cautiously toward the altar, and dreamed how it would be. She seemed frozen now, her breast rising and falling. And her face: my God, her face had twisted into a dark leer, her lips drawn back in a feral snarl to reveal her own pitiful white teeth, an expression all the more horrible in that it contained no hint of fear, but rather implied that she, too, was about to share a live meal.

"And then I understood what was happening: we were all of us drawn into the mind and will of the beast: we all looked out through its eyes, and we would all rend Chellic muscle from bone.

"I tried to withdraw. The laser was a dead weight in my right hand, desperately far away. Chellic's animal face was close now: she opened her arms wide, and advanced. Ux, with a scream that echoed round the chamber, got to his feet, but could only lean drunkenly against the slab from which his lamp illuminated the ghastly scene.

"In that moment, I got the laser up. We watched the weapon swing in our direction, and looked into the huge black hole from which the deadly burning light would erupt.

"I'll tell you what it was like, Tiel: it was as if I were pointing the weapon at myself. I looked into that muzzle as certainly as I am looking at you now. I was deathly afraid of it, but I struggled to pull the trigger all the same. I can make no claim to a heroic act, because I was even more terrified and repulsed by what would happen if I did not succeed.

"I'm not sure how to tell you the rest. Maybe you already know. Ux was also looking down the throat of the laser. And I guess it was more than he could take. He screamed and leaped toward me, distracting my tenuous aim. The weapon went off, slicing out a chunk of ceiling, and the creature seized Chellic.

"Ux hit me hard, the laser slipped away, and the mindlink dissolved. To his credit, he recovered himself almost immediately, and scrambled after the weapon. Chellic and the beast clutched each other and rotated slowly in a grim parody of a sexual embrace. Ux fired, and the creature shrieked, released her, threw a glance of pure malevolence and hatred at us, and fled into the lower levels. A second shot went wild."

He took my arm, and we walked slowly along the seafront. His palm was wet. "Ux never forgave himself."

"What happened to the woman? Chellic—?"

"She died. Died before we could get her to the surface." His grip on my arm tightened. "It was just as well."

And I thought about the inscription on the west portico, which took on a dark new meaning.

In the hour of need, I am with you.

8.

So in the end it came down to the house at the bottom of the bay.

I'd intended to be out on the Point shortly past dawn, but I woke late, after another restless night, and then delayed over a long breakfast. I had a fair notion what was waiting for me beneath that calm surface, and I was in no hurry to confront it.

I landed in thick grass near the ruined projector station. Strangely, the dome was more difficult to see up close, where its dark bronze coloring blended with the thick vegetation that overwhelmed it.

A black ragged hole had been burned through the outer shell, big enough to allow entry. I'd brought a small sculptor's laser with me, and used it to cut through the brambles. The place was half full of clay and mud. (The previous night's rain hadn't helped any.) The console had been cannibalized, and the projector was gone.

There were a few scorch marks, and the frame that would have supported the projector was cut in half.

What had Hollander said? Now the domes were better protected. Undoubtedly by something other than a physical barrier in an age where anyone could gain access to a cutting tool.

Directly across the mouth of the bay, I could see the connector station which had once formed a link with this one. It still functioned, but only in a northward direction, and was now on the outermost edge of the seawall.

After a while, I got back into the skimmer and lifted off. The bay was unsettled: there was a steady eastern chop, and the water looked rough. It was a gray, formless day, oppressive and quiet save for the steady beat of the incoming tide. I located my buoy, and circled it slowly. Uxbridge's house was not visible from the air.

A sharp gust of wind rocked the skimmer. I took it down, eased it into the water, more carefully this time, and anchored it. I did not stop to think about what lay below: I kicked off my clothes, stowed them in the aft locker, and extracted my breather from its carrying case. The lamp worked; the insert tested out. I put on a belt, hooked a utility pouch to it, strapped the depth gauge and timer to one wrist, the lamp to the other, pulled on the fins and mask, and slipped overboard.

The water was warm. But the sunless day reduced visibility severely; I could see only a few meters in natural light. I took my bearings from the buoy and the skimmer and started down.

The water turned cool, and warm again. A few fish darted away, and one of the broad-ferned swimming plants common in Fishbowl's temperate latitudes startled me by wrapping a tendril around one ankle and giving it a tug. But when I reacted, it lost interest.

The grim, mottled, sea-shrouded house gradually took shape: turrets and parapets rose out of the gray depths, stone walls formed, and oculus windows appeared and darkened, as though adjusting to a change in light.

I hovered above it for several minutes, maybe choosing my best approach, maybe hesitating. Then I descended to one of the turrets, followed its sloping roof past torn pads and exposed plates, and started down the face of the building.

At the upper level, I thumbed on my lamp and peered through a window that was, remarkably, still intact. Everything inside was covered with silt: a bed was jammed into an open doorway, light furniture had been scattered about, the contents of a bureau were spilled and buried. A closet, probably short-circuited at the time of the flooding, had partially exposed two rows of hanging garments. These fluttered gently in whatever currents passed through the room.

Below me, a long, serpentine fish glided out of a venting

pipe and disappeared into the gloom. I seized a piece of cornice and hung on until it was long gone. The stone was slippery with the algae that inhabit most water oceans.

The front door was missing, and the frame which had supported it was bent.

I passed inside, and the beam of my lamp faded into the depths of a central hall. A staircase rose on the right, and large double doors opened on the left. Again, assorted chairs and tables were tumbled about, bookcases overturned, and the whole covered with sediment. Two portraits had once hung beneath the staircase: the frames were still in place, but the canvas had shriveled in each, and no hint of the subjects remained.

Though I knew more or less where I was going, I took a moment to look through the double doors. It was a sitting room; even in its present deplorable condition, I could see that it had been a stiff, formal place: the sort of room in which one conducts formal matters, designed to impress a business acquaintance, and at the same time to hurry things along.

But I was surprised to see a photo of Ux (still dry in its frame) with several persons in academic robes. Other pictures and mementos lay buried in the silt. I knelt and dug, extracting them one by one. Most were ruined. But there were a few that had been preserved: a highly favorable review of a book he'd written on ancient languages; an award from an institution whose name was no longer legible, acknowledging his work on Mycenaean linear documents; a photo of Ux and an attractive dark-haired young woman, both in coveralls, and both wielding spades. (My God, could that be Chellic?)

I placed them carefully in my pouch.

And I found the snow photo: an enlarged duplicate of the one from the chess club. My hand shook as I brushed the last of the sand away from it. Reuben Uxbridge, wrapped in a blue parka, smiled out at me.

But the photos were in the wrong room. Jon Hollander had spoken of the retreat in the rear of the house, where he'd gone to play chess, and probably where Ux had really lived his life. That would be the normal place to keep such things. My heart pounded: I knew exactly what I was going to find. And I knew why Durell had tried to destroy the house.

There was something else about the snow photo: I examined it in the uncertain light: four men and three women in a snowstorm. Behind them, the looping colonnade of the Admin Building was visible. Just off to the left, behind Jon Hollander's head, lay the frozen rim of the pool that fronted on the Field Museum. And I knew one of the three women. The one in the middle, who was laughing, and appeared to be looking almost mischievously at Uxbridge, was the woman with the spade.

I swam the length of the hall, past closed doors, past ruined cabinets and wine sets, past the sand-clogged rubble of a lifetime. I'd acquired a few fish, fat spiny-finned creatures, that moved with me, but darted back out of the light whenever I turned it. I was grateful for their company.

I approached a door heavier and shorter than those elsewhere in the building. I pushed it ajar, and poked my lamp in.

I could see a desk, an overturned computer console, padded chairs (presumably the ones about which Hollander had spoken), and a square table. Thick drapes were still in place over the windows, and around the walls.

The inner sanctum. I caught my breath.

I used the doorknob for leverage to come upright, with my fins planted on the ground, and walked clumsily across the threshold. Things seemed somehow less displaced in that room, as though some strange gravity gripped them.

One chair had been placed precisely in the center of the floor. I looked at the circular wall, thinking vaguely of the one in the tower room. How many hours had Reuben Uxbridge sat in that chair, trying to exorcise the demon that had, indeed, followed him back from that ridden world? How often had he struck down poor bureaucratic Moss, when Moss was about to save her, save them all, at whatever cost to himself?

In a sense, Chellic had been fortunate. Uxbridge had been the real victim.

And Durell.

Only Durell, desperate for money, could supply what Uxbridge needed.

I approached the curtains, rotted now, still concealing their terrible secret, and ripped them from the wall.

In the pale glow of the lamp, the climactic struggle that Moss had described sprang to life: Chellic and the pink-eyed monstrosity, both covered with sweat, were wrapped in each other's arms, while an enraged, terrified Uxbridge, wearing a variation of the grotesque countenance I knew so well from the studio, attacked Moss. It was the instant before he reached the smaller man, when Moss was trying desperately to use the laser, when there was still time. It was the instant when Uxbridge lost his soul.

9.

I had to tell someone about it, and I decided on heroic little Casmir Moss. He was reluctant at first to see me again, thinking he'd embarrassed himself, I suppose. But in the end, he agreed to meet me for lunch, and I told him the story, the part he didn't know. When I was finished he just sat, not knowing how to respond. At last, he said simply, "It just wasn't his fault."

"Yes, it was," I said.

He looked at me, shocked. "You don't know how it was. Nobody can blame him for Chellic's death."

"Not Chellic," I said. "He wanted to relive that final moment, perhaps to change it. Or maybe he wanted to punish himself by immortalizing it. I don't know. But there was another victim besides him and Chellic. I wonder if he ever considered what he was doing to the artist . . . ?"

R.